Kicking
in
Toronto

Kicking
In
Toronto

S.R. Shuja

Second Edition

Cover page: Manzur Murad

Printed in the United States of America

Publisher: Mind Talkers Publishing

ISBN #:978-0-9878187-6-8

Visit www.mindtalkers.com

To Canada

Contents

A Trial for Spider-Man

Some of the most noticeable structures in Scarborough, a Toronto suburb and part of Greater Toronto Area (GTA), are its multi-storied apartment buildings. Since we decided to immigrate to Canada from Bangladesh, hoping to offer a better future to our next generation, things were never the same. The long journey from Dhaka to Toronto that included eighteen hours of flying time was the longest we had ever travelled. The new life in our new country was overwhelming by every means. The hoops that we had to jump over just to be able to rent a small apartment on the twenty-second floor of one of those high rise buildings was a true awakening. Back in Dhaka, a computer programmer working for a multinational company, my life wasn't particularly appalling. Despite enjoying healthy remuneration I was proudly living with my parents, in their three storied house, along with my wife Shili and infant son Zaki. Housing in Dhaka – a bustling, sprawling, traffic congested and crime infested city of tens of millions of people - is expensive, though not out of reach for well established professionals. Nevertheless, my parents insisted us to live with them. Traditionally it is not considered embarrassing. Our new apartment in Scarborough, just five floors beyond the roof, was literally the first home that we ever considered as truly ours.

The first day in the apartment was kind of scary; especially the attached balcony with four feet high concrete railing with several noticeable cracks was not something that we considered safe. I suffered from acrophobia, to elaborate - any height more than thirty feet sent me to a shock, my feet trembled, visibly, my head spun uncontrollably. As I still braved to take a peek below leaning over the balcony it seemed that the building was bending forward and I was about to lose my footing and slid down to the guaranteed death. I sprung back inside the apartment never again to indulge myself with such luxury. My better half had a laughing feat on my expense. She was exceptionally courageous for an otherwise timid woman and height had no impact on her. Yet, when I bolted and locked the balcony door making it essentially inaccessible she didn't object. A few days later we found a flock of pigeons had snatched away the opportunity and made several nests there. This, once we allowed ourselves to get used to the foul smell of the abundant droppings, quickly turned out to open up a window to the nature. Eggs were laid; babies were born, right in front of our keen eyes. Never before had I thought looking out through a bedroom window would offer the nature at its best so up close, right in our backyard - in a way.

Like all multi-storied apartment buildings in this part of the town ours was home of six to seven hundred families, surpassing total number of apartments by a large margin as many of the apartments were happy nests of multiple families, usually blood related. One mover had once told me that during one of his jobs he had found six families living in an apartment – no bigger than one thousand square feet. He swore that he counted twenty-two people - ten adults and twelve kids. At first it sounded ridiculous and heavily exaggerated but later we realized it was a common case in areas like Scarborough where South East Asian people flocked. While many could find it tough to digest we had little difficulty understanding the concept behind this. Save, save and save. After a few years most bought houses and moved out of the apartment buildings permanently. The savings definitely showed the path of prosperity. However, the inevitable question might rise - why the building management allowed it? After all, the three page finely printed rental contracts clearly stated that only and only one family could live in the rented property, the apartment. The answer was simple. Lately many renters were moving to houses, thanks to low interests, competitive housing market and less stringent buying requirements, the apartment rental business wasn't as good as it used to be.

Years passed by quickly. Things had never been easy since we landed here but it moved. Life went on amid all the struggle that we experienced in this new world, as I tried to find my way through the confusing job market with its clearly discriminatory unwritten corporate policies that frequently overlooked highly educated and experienced new immigrants for suitable positions. I attended evening classes after my regular day time restaurant job where I worked as a busboy. I had come a long way from being snobby about low paying jobs and now saw it as an intermediate steps to my ultimate goal – a corporate official job. Uh! How much I missed sitting on a comfortable revolving chair working on a computer. Life was different here but not unacceptable. As I saw my tips at work grow gradually to a level where it was healthy enough to contribute in my expenses the inevitable idea of owning a house emerged spontaneously. Not a day passed by when we didn't discuss the possibility and even dared to browse through the colorful booklets the housing developers dropped in plentiful on the floor of the building lobby.

It was hard not to. After a few years in a congested apartment, it was just natural that a sane mind would look for better viable options that offered more freedom and flexibility. There was definitely a hidden satisfaction in living among a population that offered diversity at its best - a true melting pot, but it also came with its share of problems. People showed a general tendency to ignore the simpler things of life like compassion, cleanliness and mutual respect. It barely surprised anybody when last night's leftover from pizza to meat loaves found their way to the stairs, elevators, and corridors. Shili swore that she had once smelled even human urine on the staircase. There was a garbage Shute on each floor but strangely enough the garbage always piled up around it, often high enough to initiate a reluctant visit by one of the grudging building maintenance crews. In addition, there was this ominous presence of noise pollution that had become an inseparable part of our lives. Waking up at three in the morning only to discover that the undue interruption was due to a cranked up music box in the neighborhood had become a regular thing. Once upon a time I loved romantic Hindi songs — the Gazals. The continuous overdose that I received for years from the Gazal lover who lived right under me had up-rooted my passion for all love songs. And then there was that endless agony with the elevators. The building had three of them - one never worked, the other one frequently revolted forcing the third one to bear the enormous load. Waiting half an hour to board an elevator had become way of life.

One night, once Zaki went to sleep, we — man and woman — called for an emergency meeting.

"How long like this?" Shili barked. She had to wait twenty minutes for the elevator just that morning while Zaki screamed his head off.

"What do you want me to do?" I asked innocently.

"What's that suppose to mean?" She snapped. "How many times have I told you to buy a house?"

I shrugged. "It takes money; a lot of it."

"I heard we could buy one with just 3% down payment." She had done her home work.

"True, but we'll have head full of grey hairs before we pay our loan off. The interest would be a killer." I spoke my mind loudly.

"If we wait we'll have grey hairs even before buying one." She shot back.

"We need to save some money to put larger down payment. You can't have it all."

That was a blunder.

"What did you just say? Are you suggesting I squander? Have you seen what the other wives do? You dare to say things like that because I am so considerate..."

Sometime later, after plenty of loving words and a dose of my especial romantic routine when she finally calmed down the night had progressed further down in its path to dawn. We were both tired, discouraged. None of us wanted to dive into a situation that promised overwhelming financial burden. We decided to resort to more imprudence and as a result hoped to enlarge our savings. There was no other way to do it. Shili looked awfully determined and even took the effort to create a balance book right then with the columns neatly drawn and the headers nicely written. Every expense had to be noted and categorized. For any saving strategy to work we needed to understand our expenditure better, we both agreed, a rare occurrence.

The first few weeks went trouble free. We stuck to our plan and diligently listed all expenses under categories like housing, grocery, entertainment etc. We even drew up a plan to cut back our entertainment budget to nil and grocery costs to half starting from the following month. You had to give up something to achieve something. We both understood that. The spirit was strong, determination was sky high. That's when the trouble started. It came abruptly, giving us little chance to prepare.

We bought our groceries from the local Food Basic store, once or twice a week. Zaki, who was now four, took especial interest in fruits. This was very pleasing to us, considering how many kids were hooked to high calorie fatty foods and struggled to keep their weights off well before they could spell the word 'weight'. Fruits, in the contrary, had fewer calories and had beneficial vitamins – a great combination. However, the following week our visit to the grocery store took an unwanted turn. We had happily stuffed our cart with apples, grapes and nectarines, Zaki's favorites, and moved on to the cereal section. Mother and son both feasted on cereal after sunrise, unlike me, who had to wait well into the day to build up an appetite for food. Defying all laws of healthy life style I had diligently ignored breakfast, practically all my adult life. As a result, this cereal episode was something that was very personal to the duo, while I browsed through jelly and jam section, checking out calorie contents, one of my hobbies.

They both knew what they wanted and usually zoomed through the cereal aisle. Not this time. When ten minutes had passed and the duo didn't show up I became suspicious and walked to the neighboring aisle to check on them. Soon I found the two engaged in a tug of war over a cereal box, the son hung to it with his arms wrapped around it tightly while his mother tried to pull it away from him. What was that all about? I felt the need to mediate. Zaki had picked a cereal that he wasn't used to eat, Shili explained, he still wanted it only based upon the fact that it had some worthless pictures of a so called super hero. A good look at the colorful box revealed the ultimate truth – it was surrounded with flashy pictures of Spider-Man. Since the first Spider-Man movie had rocked the moviegoers the market had been flooded with prod-ucts that bore the images of the splendid superhero in his fascinating red and blue costume in eye catching poses. Obviously the mother had little patience for such pretentious display. The son, on the other hand, looked just about ready to declare a full war over it.   As if to prove his intentions beyond any reasonable doubt he brought in his awfully strong lungs in the battle and started to scream at the top of his voice.

"I want Spider man! I want Spider man!"

Shili tried to reason, "Don't be a fool. That is just a picture. The serial that comes inside that box is no good."

Zaki wasn't letting such useless logic to deviate him.

"I want Spider-Man!" He howled.

Shili shrugged in utter frustration and looked at me for help. Oh no, not me. If anybody was looking bad for troubling a cute little guy let that be the rude, thoughtless mother. The dad would rather accept the role of a nice, smiling man with a heart of gold.

"Let him have it." I said, indulgently.

Son smiled at me like the way sun comes out from behind the cloud after a rainy morning. Who knew that tiny victory would soon come back to haunt us? When we realized the mistake it was already too late.

The following weekend we visited one of my old friends house to celebrate his only son Joy's fifth birth-day. It had been a little while since we had had an oppor-tunity to be in their presence. However, in our busy lives a few months gap wasn't totally unacceptable. We spoke on the phone and regularly wrote electronic mails. We stayed in touch. Nevertheless, this time around, as we stepped inside their house we realized things had changed, quite drastically, something neither of us expected, Shili or me. We were clearly surprised and quietly shaken as we noticed the ubiquitous presence of the dreaded Spider-Man, posters to figures - in all size and shape, from walls to the floors. The indulging parents, no different than us, had planned an all Spider-Man birthday, and to make it a true success had bought everything Spider-Man – from toy cars, costumes, hats to table cover, paper plates and even the napkins.

We were truly terrified. Zaki and Joy were close. With the exception of short living skirmishes every five minutes they were otherwise ideal friends. We knew this barren display of Mr. Spider-Man was bound to imprint a deep impression on Zaki's young mind, one kids passion was about to be passed onto another. I felt hopeless. Why were some parents so inconsiderate? I wondered. My friend did well as a software developer. Perhaps it was his way of declaring success to the world. He had the strength to bring the coveted super hero to his young child – there was a clear sign of ego in it.   Regardless, I couldn't stop wondering how these companies were even allowed to allure such innocent kids with their provocative marketing efforts. Why did we have governments? What were they so busy doing when such injustice continued?

There's no shame in admitting that what I felt bubbling up inside my mind could be passed on as contempt, as I apprehensively observed the quick lessons that Zaki received from Joy. We made it a point to cut short our visit with a lame excuse and got ourselves out of there before much damage could be done.

Couple of days had passed by quietly. Fearfully we stayed watchful. No nagging or pleading for Spider-Man toys yet. We relaxed with a sigh of relief. Perhaps he was too young to totally absorb the idea of an enchanting super hero.

Winter was approaching quickly. Zaki's last year's winter jacket didn't fit him anymore. Few days later we went to the nearby shopping mall in the evening. Shili was a picky shopper, often navigated through store to store for that perfect something, obviously me with a tired Zaki on my shoulder shadowing her. Hours passed by while Shili struggled to choose a winter jacket for Zaki, frequently demanding my honest opinion and rejecting even when I gave my full approval, which was every time she asked. We travelled from Sears to Bay to old Navy, without luck. She was determined not to give up and we continued in our endless journey from store to store.

Suddenly we noticed in front of a specialty clothing store a five-six year old boy of Chinese descent was rolling on the ground as he cried and screamed at the top of his voice. His helpless parents looked at each other, clearly in total loss in the face of such hysteric act. It didn't take too long for a crowd to gather around, curiosity and compassion flew in abundance. The attendants from the clothing store scurried out to investigate. Soon the mystery was revealed. The boy had just been in that store and picked a tee shirt with an image of Spider man, which he pleaded his parents to purchase for him. When that went unheeded he resorted to something that worked. The parents jointly added that the boy already had two shirts with almost similar printed pictures. Every time he saw another one with slightly different color variation he demanded to have it.

A group of elderly shoppers had joined us to the show. The heart wrenching cry and all that rolling and shaking proved too much for them. While most limited their sympathy into deep sighs and wet eyes a few decided to speak up and appeal for the unfortunate boy.

"Come on guys. Get him the shirt. How expensive can that be?" An elderly woman was the first one to plead.

I stole a quick glimpse at the price tag. Thirty five dollars. With tax it would be a little over forty. Not a negligible amount by any means. Grandma, if your heart breaks for the poor boy so much then why don't you buy it for him? I thought.

The sales girls who worked in the store were young. All this screaming and commotion and the crowd that gathered outside the store started to make them a bit nervous. Not knowing how else to handle the situation, even they started to gently press the helpless parents of the boy who continued with his tantrum, perhaps with more vigor, now that he had a house full of spectators.

"Get him what he wants, please." The girls pleaded. "If this goes on for too long we'll lose our customers. "

"Someone might call the police." Another girl cleverly added.

Possibly the word 'Police' did the trick. Many new immigrants are wary of the legal complexities and fears the wrath of the law man could fall on them for apparently harmless reasons. Especially the myths about losing children to the social services on the basis of child neglect and abuse is a fearsome one. Nobody in their sane mind wants to get into trouble with law on that ground. The helpless parents gave up and paid for the tee shirt. The distressed boy recovered instantly; up on his foot he held the tee shirt high with a victory dance, his joy rippled through the crowd, forcing spontaneous smiles into the satisfied faces of grandma and grandpas.

The parents gave away a thin, meaningless smile before quickly pulling the boy away from the store and the crowd.

I had just let go a breath of relief when I felt a gentle pull on my hand. It was Zaki.

"Dad?"

I coughed. "Yes?"

"I want that shirt too. Jonny have two of them."

Shili was about to roll her eyes and lash out at him when I whispered to her "Did you like that show?" She struggled to keep her cool. Zaki wasn't known to put up a tantrum but there was no guarantee that it wouldn't start right there. We had just seen how stupid the parent's looked. We did as asked.

Once we were back in the car, our dear son had quickly changed into his newly bought tee shirt and was smilingly ear to ear. I forced a smile while his mother glared at him. "Blackmailer!" She muttered.

Zaki had been going to school since last September. This was Zaki's first time away from home without any of his parents being with him. Shili was a stay home mom and there was no reason to put him to daycare. We weren't sure how he would do in school. He was one of the youngest kids in his class. Nevertheless, to our amazement we found him to be very happy at school. While the bigger kids returned home with teary eyes, he was always full of excitement. This in turn gave me something to tease his mother.

"He must have been bored to death in your company. Now I rarely see him complaining."

The mother gave me a fiery glance.

"Don't talk silly. How many hours in a day do you spend with him? For the few hours he stays in school I get some rest as well."

I wiped of the smile and somberly said, "Didn't we have a plan for half a dozen kids?"

I had to run to escape from the attack of her deadly pinches.

"What do you take me for?" She lashed out. "Do you think I would spend all my life just raising kids? I have good education. I'll look for a job."

We both knew her Masters degree in Botany from Dhaka University wasn't going to be good enough for her to find a job here. If she wanted to work in the area of her interest she had to go back to school.

Anyway, as we started to get really comfortable with Zaki going to school something worrisome happened. One day he came back from school with tears rolling down his cheek like a pair of spring creeks. His mom was devastated. School was about ten minutes walking distance from home. Shili walked him back and forth to school. On their way back home Zaki sobbed unstoppably all through the way. A lot of pleading later the mystery was revealed. One of his class mates had a Spider man bag and he didn't. Why didn't he? As soon as I returned home from my work I was faced with this universal question – why the other boy had something that he didn't, especially when it was something as wonderful as a spider man bag? I must have hesitated to find a suitable answer because son took up the opportunity to decide his next action. "Dad, you have to buy me that bag now."

I coughed. "It's too late. All stores are closed."

"You are lying. We went the other night. All stores were open." He instantly replied.

Never undermine the intelligence of these little people. Next we reasoned, scolded, pleaded, begged – nothing worked. Instead he started to cry. He had to have the spider man bag or he couldn't possibly go to school the next day. Shili got upset and yelled some with no impact. Finally we ran out of patience and headed to the mall. Luckily we found a similar bag. Once purchased son held it dearly, smiling with all his teeth revealed. There went some more of our planned savings.

At the end of the month, once Zaki went to bed, we husband and wife got our balance book out. We had listed all our expenses diligently for all through the month. We spent hours grouping the expenses into distinct categories to get a clear picture of our costs. Rent – $1050, grocery – $405, Car insurance and gas – $310 ... Most of it was usual expenses. There was no way to do without them. But the category that instantly got our attention was something very disturbing. Spider-Man – $220.

In Toronto if a middle class family with one income could save four-five hundred dollars at the end of each month they had a lot of reason to consider themselves lucky. This was especially true for the new immigrants who almost invariably engaged in low paying jobs as I was. In addition the federal and provincial taxes were kind of high in Canada, and there was that ever presenting effect of rising prices of essentials. In the midst of it all, the new troublemaker namely Mr. Spider-Man, wasn't welcomed, obviously. Shili and I exchanged grim glances. After some more basic mathematics we found our saving last month was 158 dollars.

Mili grimaced. "If we move at this speed, I'll be ninety before we have enough money to put up 25% down payment for even a rotten shed."

I bitterly said, "Forget the house for now. We need to have a strategy to beat this Spider-Man guy."
She shrugged in frustration. "After Spider-Man there will be some other man. Everybody is aiming at the tiny disposable income that we have. There are no places to run."

I threw away the balance book. What was the use of all these calculations?

I stealthily checked out my better half. There was no immediate objection. I quietly let go a deep breath of relief. Spider-Man was bugging me, admitted. Nevertheless, I couldn't stop myself from thanking him just a tiny bit. There couldn't possibly be anything more boring than trying to balance your finances. When all these giant corporations were failing left and right why a minuscule speck like me was even bothering to do the unthinkable?

Thank you Spider-Man! I quietly rejoiced my new

found freedom. All charges are dropped. You are free to go.

Agawa Canyon

Several years ago I went to Sue St. Marie with a year-long contract job. About seven hundred kilometers away from Toronto this town has two parts, the larger section is part of Canada and the smaller of USA. They are separated by a body of water with a giant suspended bridge connecting the two. There is a lock here which connects Lake Superior with Lake Huron. At both ends there are several tour boats offering water rides for a hefty fee. The major attraction in the Canadian side, however, is the Agawa Canyon train trip. Tourists come from all around the world to take this trip, especially during fall season.

Since we came to Sue St. Marie we had been looking for an opportunity to take this trip. It finally happened in the middle of June. The posted fares for such trips are understandably high, for adults it was close to $60 and for kids something like $25. In June the tour organizers suddenly dropped the fares to half of the posted rates for the locals only. The offer was valid for only two days. As a result the lines in front of the usually barren counters turned kilometer long. With the exception of summer and fall these counters rarely see any visitors. Especially during September and October - official fall season – a healthy crowd of visitors, mostly Americans, take this trip to enjoy the beautiful fall color of the Northern Ontario. No wonder, that is also the time when showing due diligence the Canadian tour operators hikes the fair up.

The platform to board the tour train is near the river called St. Mary's Rapid that flows along the town. The train was scheduled to leave at 8 AM in the morning. We woke up early, got ready in a flash, packed up some food and showed up in the station by 7 AM – a little too determined not to miss the train. A large crowd was expected hence going early also meant convenient parking. To our surprise, despite such early arrival, we found the platform overflowing with people. Any doubts about effectiveness of price cuts can be thrown into oblivion.

In this town of almost eighty thousand inhabitants we were only two families from Bangladesh – us and Rajib family. Rajib bhai (brother), a senior friend of mine from the same educational institution in Bangladesh, had been living in the town with his wife and a daughter for almost four years. He was a lecturer in the local Sue College. After immigrating to Canada from England he had gone through some difficult times and ended up in this distant town in the north western Ontario landing this teaching job. He eventually made up his mind to make it his home. The series of events that got us together were quite unique.

Since coming to Sue about four months ago we met many people but none from South East Asia – a particular interest of Mili. Approaching Eid-ul-fitr, the celebration that Muslims perform after Ramadan – a month for fasting, in her quest to have a customary celebration with other fellow Muslims Mili took a desperate measure. She picked up the Telephone guide and compiled a list of Muslim names focusing primarily on anything that sounded Bangladeshi. The name Rajib sounded familiar – prompting her to pick up the phone. Bull's eye! It turned out that not only he was from Bangladesh but he also had the misfortune to lecture my class during my University years – though very briefly. Due to my scarce presence in classes my recollection of him was practically nothing. I learned that he had secured a commonwealth scholarship and flew to England to pursue higher studies. Curious, I inquired with two of my class mates who lived in Toronto. Both knew Rajib bhai like the back of their hands and subtly cast doubt about my sanity for not remembering him.

Rajib bhai and his family – wife Nusrat and daughter Lota - made it to the station just before five minutes to eight. To their relief the start time had already been pushed back indefinitely as additional cars were being added to accommodate all the people who convened. Rajib bhai's elderly parents lived with him who were not accompanying them in this trip. Since we met them we sensed some sort of ongoing trouble. Nusrat bhabi (sister-in-law) did not want to live here in social isolation and was eager to move back to Toronto. However, Rajib bhai had no interest in leaving his current job. We found them engaging into heated arguments quite often.

Lota was six and highly restless. At every opportunity she would zoom away in random direction. It was quite difficult to manage her. When in her company Zaki acted the same way. He was couple of years younger than Lota but was equally troublesome. Their combined

25

disturbances could annoy the most patient.

After plenty of dilly-dallying finally when the long, well built train left the station it was already nine in the morning. The cars were specious with large high back seats that could be swivelled to seat face to face or back to back. We occupied couple of rows of these chairs and set them up to allow us to seat facing each other.

It was a beautiful day. The bright sun had risen in the eastern sky lighting up the earth with its beautiful and warm rays. Unfortunately the heat from the rays might have been a little too much for comfort as they shone right on our faces. Little distracted but not discouraged by any means we soon found the natural beauty that surrounded us as we advanced through the woods was more than enough to filter out the mild discomfort.

Agawa Canyon is a name given by the native Indians, which meant hidden port. It isn't difficult to figure out the reason for such naming. There are literally very few routes to visit this area. In the year 1899 Algoma Central Railway had connected the mining towns in the North Central Ontario to the towns near Great lakes like Sault St. Marie and Michipicoten Harbor. The 516 kilometer railway ended in Herst. In 1997 Algoma Steel Company announced the closure of their mining activities in Wawa, as a result since 1998 that specific part of the railway remained unused. Recently only the tour train was operating.

Agawa Canyon is 180 kilometers north of Sault St. Marie. It would take the train to reach there about four hours, arriving around 1 in the afternoon. We would be given couple of hours to hike around in the canyon. With another four-hour return trip we would reach Sault by 7 PM. There would still be some daylight left. Everything looked just perfect. The environment inside the train was quite festive, as one might imagine. Lota and Zaki had packed up and were running up and down the car adding up to the commotion that was already ongoing. Half the passengers were kids, mostly young and understandably noisy, hence nobody really cared. Shili had tried to stop the two with a few scolding but the impact of that was too short living to claim any success. Rajib bhai and Nusrat bhabi sat side by side but from their heavy posture it was clear that they were not in talking terms. They looked in opposite directions.

Our train advanced in a slow pace, through the greeneries of the densely grown woods and startling groups of birds, leaving behind the city limits of Sault Ste. Marie. Lakes of all sizes and shapes ran past us with their glittering blue water. The bright sun blinded us every now and then as the train meandered through the land that rose and dropped in random intervals with the view changing frequently.

Things had been very joyous inside the train, filled with dreamy appreciations. The adults leaned against their seats and enjoyed leisurely the beautiful views while the kids ran around with pure excitement. I had tagged along both the still and video cameras with me and kept myself busy taking images of both kinds. Left, right, up, down. "How many pictures are you going to take of the same stuff?" Shili snapped.

I gave her a crooked look. What a foolish girl! How could two views be same? Click! Click! Click!

Later the train rolled over an embankment on the

Montreal River. There is a wooden bridge over the river. This is one of the most anticipated parts of the trip that is advertised heavily with its image popping up in many places. Everybody wait for this particular part of the trip with their cameras ready. We were no exception to that rule. As soon as we saw the train approaching the bridge everybody stood up and crowded against the windows. The train slowed down to allow the passengers to enjoy that extremely beautiful view to its entirety. Click! Click! Click! The train rumbled slowly toward the foot of the bridge as we looked out with bursting eyes determined not to let go this most remarkable view of water, forest and sky smoothly merging into each other. I noticed Rajib bhai and Nusrat bhabi glanced at each other quickly before looking out through the windows. This was good sign. There's little doubt that we all are the children of nature and it can do magic in our lives. To make things groovier I took two quick snapshot of Shili at the back-drop of this natural wonder. She gave me a hard look. "Why are you wasting the films? There's still a long way to go."

I laughed out loudly, for no apparent reason. My mind sung away – *I am so crazy for you my love!* I had the habit of writing sound-alike songs of Tagor and Nazrul – two legendary songwriters of Bengali language.

Almost four hours later, causing a major commotion in the peaceful mountainside, our train moved from the last glimpse of the Highway seven and Lake Superior, and started to climb down the canyon face. *Chug chug, chug chug, choooo chooooooooo.* Moments later we were rewarded with the most amazing view that I have ever seen as the train slowed down into a valley with lush greeneries, several midsize waterfalls and a creek flowing right through it. Everybody seemed to be mesmerized with the sheer beauty of that sudden discovery. As soon as the train stopped everybody raced to climb out of the train. It had a planned stoppage here for couple of hours only. There were a lot to do and nobody wanted to waste time.

Shili, Zaki and I rushed out of the train as well. Rajib bhai along with Nusrat bhabi and Lota was right behind us. There was no shortage of smiles in their faces. Nusrat bhabi's gloomy face had turned bright in joy. She even tried to hold Rajib bhai's hand avoiding our eyes. Rajib bhai was a shy man. He got out of the hand lock and put his hands inside his pockets. Finding Zaki and Lota sprinting toward the creek I ran after them. Both of them had severe likeness for water bodies. Once grabbing them I made my way to the washrooms where there were already pretty long line ups. Men and women had separate facilities. There was a souvenir store and several food shops next to the washrooms. I am the owner of a very active bladder. Sight of a washroom was sure to excite it. This time it was no exception.

Once all of us had taken care of our bladders we started for the Canyon walk. This place was created almost 1 billion years ago. There are three waterfalls in close proximity of varying sizes and a lookout point about 250 feet above. For the convenience of the visitors several trails have been created that go in loops touching various attraction points. We started in one direction, Rajib bhai and family started on the opposite direction. Once we were done with our sightseeing we'd meet back in the train.

We checked out Beaver falls (175 feet), Bridal Veil falls (225 feet) and a third one located at the end of the Otter creek trail. Bridal Veil was the most beautiful out of the three. Shili was so taken by its beauty that she did something very unusual. "Take a snapshot of me here." She demanded. "Zaki, please come here. Stand with me." Mother and son stood in a terrific pose, all ready for the snapshot. As I picked up the camera I noticed there were no more films left. Talk about trouble! I bought two reels of 24 films but brought only one reel which I already used up on our way to the canyon. I forgot the second reel at home.

"No film, right?" Shili snapped. "When I want to take a snapshot you run out of films? The moment I ask for something you have issues. Last time when we went to Montreal...."

In the next half an hour as we walked back I was forced to remember many forgotten facts. A simple mistake opened up the door to a deluge of troublesome memories. Zaki had covered his ears with his palms. Every few moments he would ask anxiously, "Mom, who are you scolding? Dad, right? Not me."

Leaving them behind I started to climb up the wooden stairs of the lookout trail all the way up to 250 feet. Shili stayed back at the ground level with Zaki. The beautiful view that extended up to the horizon was spectacular. Time was short. Train would leave in as little as twenty minutes. We would have to walk considerable length to return to the train. I quickly climbed down. Rajib family had completed their sightseeing and joined Mlli and Zaki at the bottom of the stairs. They smiled at me as I came rushing down.

30

"Why didn't you tell me that you ran out of films?" Rajib bhai said. "I still have many left."

"A total nut!" Shili said. "He wasted all the films in the train taking useless snapshots."

Very objectionable remark. I acted as if I did not hear that. On our way back to the train we lined up on the green fields by the creek as Rajib bhai took several snapshots of us with his camera. There was a small wooden bridge over the creek. We took several group photos standing over it. Click! Click!

Many old folks had brought food with them. They sat by the creek leisurely and ate their packed lunches. Clearly it weren't their first time in this trip. We were all very hungry. Once returned into the train we attacked our own food supplies – things that we had packed in bags.

Train started back soon. Another four hours of journey ahead. All the eyes were glued outside through the windows with many ready with their cameras. The train climbed up the canyon wall very slowly leaving behind the beautiful dreamy valley and ran through dense forest. Slowly, everybody gave a rest to the cameras and relaxed back into their seats in attempts to get a sleep. The trip went quite well with sightseeing, pictures and the nice hike in the valley. Now it was time to return home. Most were tired, some sleepy.

The ending of this trip didn't go very well though. After about half way down we were told that there was some kind of problem with the line. Our train could advance but would have to go in a very slow pace. And slow it was! The kids took a long nap and once awake asked the inevitable question, "Are we home yet?"

Nobody answered.

"I knew something like this was going to happen." Shili eventually lost her cool and said in deep resentment. "After all we are in the company of the inauspicious man." Of course that would be me. I was quite hurt. *I am so crazy for you my love, how could you hurt me in such a way?* I sung in my mind. I wasn't still sure whether I would sing it in Tagor's tune or Nazrul's tune.

The four hour return trip ended in seven hours. When we finally reached Sault St. Marie it was 10 PM. Tired, bitter and sleepy passengers lethargically climbed down the train to the platform. Who thought such a wonderful experience would end in this nightmare. The Tour authority apologized for the inconvenience and offered rain checks to anybody who wanted to take the trip again, for no charge.

We did not return for the trip but when one of my friends had visited us with his family we gave them the tickets. They took the trip and were equally amazed. The feeling was very satisfying.

An Afternoon with Hashem Family

We hadn't visited Trina and her family for a while. Her father Hashem - a small, skinny and cheerful man – was my wife Shili's distant cousin. However, he was hardly the reason why we eagerly planned for such visits. He had three daughters: Trina the oldest was ten, Pushpa six and Urmila three. Couple of years ago when Hashem family had first arrived in Toronto we rushed to see them. That was my first meeting with the family and Shili's after a long time. Hashem bhai (brother) had been away from Bangladesh, our home country, and was working in Malaysia as a teaching faculty in a university. During that first meeting in Toronto both of us – husband and wife – were quiet taken by the three cute and angelic girls. We had always desired our first child to be a precious and patient girl but instead we were blessed with a boy – Zaki, who was now four – and accepted him with all his tantrums and restiveness.

Hashem bhai, a dream host, were known to go a distance to treat his guests. You ask for a mere glass of water and he would bring you a feast. Shili wasn't much for such excessiveness and every time she caught him going overboard she furrowed her brows and scolded, "Hashem bhai, don't be a show off. I can't tolerate that at all."

Hasham bhai had known her since she was a little girl herself and had clearly been very affectionate. Her every scolding kicked off varieties of wide smiles accompanied by a sure display of paper white teeth.

Shili found it even further annoying. "What's the smile for?" She was sure to snap.

This usually made him break into high pitched laughter.

Anyway, on this fine July afternoon, a Saturday, we dropped by at Hashem family's two bedroom apartment in Mississauga on a short notice to wish Puspha a happy birthday and hand over the gift that Shili had purchased for her.

Couple of months ago we had received a special invitation in the occasion of Pushpa's sixth birthday where we could not attend as I had to travel to Montreal on a project work. After returning home I heard the day was celebrated with plenty of fun stuff. Trina and her sisters loved to dance. Their mother Julekha bhabi (sister-in-law) had a fascination for cultural stuff. In her youth she was known to have taken lessons in music and dancing. She tried her best to pass on her skill to her daughters. However, that probably wasn't quite needed. Owing to all the Bollywood musical style movies which are so ubiquitous in our homes that even the little ones learn how to dance Indian style even before they can walk straight. By the time they are past toddler age the girls are already dressing up and acting up like the beautiful and glamorous Bollywood heroines.

Trina and the sisters had a few apprentices. There was a family from North West part of Bangladesh who lived in the same floor. Their eight year old daughter Daisy was a diehard fan of Trina. She was known to spend most part of her days in this apartment.

Najra, who was six or seven, lived at the floor right above. They were from Pakistan. Both of her parents used to work during the day; hence after school Najra stayed with Trina until evening when her parents returned. According to Julekha bhabi she (Najra) was so comfortable in this apartment that most days she didn't want to go home.

Trina's Cultural club consisted of Daisy, Najra, Pushpa, Urmila and of course herself. It had already been brought to our attention that the girls not only gained expertise in Indian dancing but had also acquired essential skill set in acting as well. Due to our absence in the grand event - Pushpa's birthday party - we had missed out the especial show that the girls had presented. Our visit seemed to have given the gang a chance to re-enact the whole celebration. Not only we ended up watching the one and a half hour long video of the birthday party in its entirety but soon found out that the talented group was preparing to repeat part of the show in our honour. At this development I felt quite worried fearing this could eventually worn me out but outside I remained all smile – ear to ear.

Trina and her team went on to spend a good half an hour only to dress up. Colourful dance outfits called *ghagra* were yanked out of the closets where they were hung from sturdy hangers and after some shuffle and scuffle among the younger ones to sort out who was going to wear what things eventually calmed down though not before the peace was shattered briefly with the howling of Urmila. They rehearsed for a little while behind the closed door of one of the two bedrooms.

In the meantime Julekha bhabi went on to start her very own cooking bonanza with the kids favourites pulao (butter rice) and korma (butter chicken) – two special preparations. It took little imagination to realize where she might have gotten the idea from. Sensing Shili's wrath was about to fall on him Hashem bhai skillfully allowed himself out of the apartment mumbling something about inviting parents of Daisy and Najra to dine with us. Both families worked during weekends and there were little chance of them showing up – we thought. Not so, not today. It must have been some sort of auspicious day because both families were docked at home. Our original plan of dropping by for a short visit had now all but gone. Anticipation of a grand meal, the ensuing cultural show, friendly chitchat with Hashem bhai and his two friends I had just met - everything was going just great. Though, the bright summer sun outside tried its best to excite me, rebuking silently for anchoring inside the four walls when I could be outdoor, enjoying the warmth of the short living season. I needed little tanning as one might already guessed but I was addicted to the sun and my summer days spent mostly outside. I pulled my attention off the sun and waited patiently for the show. We were already too deep into it and leaving wasn't an option any more.

As the bedroom door where the rehearsal was going on in full speed opened slightly to allow us a glimpse into it I found the girls chasing Zaki, clearly their attempt to have him slip into a ghagra wasn't going too smoothly as he vehemently protested declaring repeatedly that he was a boy and was not about to put on a girly stuff. Then somebody cranked the music up and the door closed – to my relief. I hated loud music. It was nice to find out that at least the children were having a great time.

Daisy's father, Muhabbot Ali, was an easygoing, fun loving man. Even before we had been fully introduced he started cracking jokes in his local dialect, every time breaking into uncontrollable laughter. Not fully knowing that particular dialect I barely understood what he was saying but still wanted to be polite and half heartedly chuckled which sounded more like snorts.

Najra's parents Niaz Muhammed and Nazma had the looks of devout Muslims. Niaz was middle aged, mild mannered and wore a long beard. Nazma wore pitch black burqa that covered practically all her body except a small gap where her eyes were. She had quickly disappeared inside one of the bedrooms and I did not even hear her voice. Imagining how she must have been feeling under that fully covered garb in a hot day like that I was slightly taken aback. Muhabbot brought me back to reality with his loud laughter. Must be another of his jokes.

Finding Niaz who didn't even speak the same language chuckling happily I looked at him curiously. "I do not understand a word," he responded, "but I still laugh because it makes Muhabbot bhai happy."

Muhabbot overheard it and didn't look very happy about it. As a result he tried to translate his jokes into English. But his English was only a slight improvement from his Bengali dialect. After struggling for a little he gave up on his jokes and engaged in small talks. Hashem bhai translated as needed basis and we were able to make a meaningful conversation. I learned that Muhabbot was a big businessman back home. Since immigrating to Canada he had started a food store. The business was sort of okay but they had to work hard. Between husband and wife they spent most part of their days in the store. Sometimes two young girls came to work for them. Today was one of those days.

Niaz was part of higher management of a large drug company back home. Since they came here he was working as a night guard in an office building located in downtown Toronto. Not a bad job for a new immigrant but not something he wanted to continue doing too long. He was taking a course on Quality control and was hoping to get an office job when done.

Trina appeared at one point and interrupted our discussion to declare that the cultural show was about to start and we were to applaud for the performers.

Before the applaud had stopped the air filled with the sweet sound of the ghungur (ankle bracelet) as the performers danced in unison to the stage – the tiny space between the TV and the sofas in the living room where we sat - and started their first dancing routine. Zaki and Urmila were about to ruin the whole dance with their inexperience – to put it modestly - and were quickly taken out of the pack, which actually backfired as they screamed and shouted in protest forcing the whole show to a halt. Taken aback with this unexpected development Trina had to unwillingly cut short the planned program to make room for a talent show to allow the agitated toddlers an opportunity to show their materials. Urmila was the first one to take the stage and instantly won the audience with her stumbling dancing moves.

Zaki had a general tendency to go against the wind and when his turn came he refused to perform and declared he would instead draw something. Once he was supplied with paper and pencil he drew something that one could pass as a distant cousin of Spider-Man. He had been an avid fan of the Spidey and drew all sorts and sizes of frescos of him inside our apartment. I must say he had improved over the years, thankfully, considering we had to bear the unsightly walls. His mother however was not very happy with this artistic ability. There is this consensus among many that the connection between an artist and addiction to drugs is given.

"He is definitely going to be a big artist someday," Pushpa affectionately said.

I could see Shili's face clouding. Not a chance.

Finally, it was dinner time, my favourite activity. Recently as I started to grow a love handle Shili had been quite critical of me and food. She had very keen eyes and could detect tiny differences in my size and shape. Careful not to fall on her radar I stealthily ate to the content of my heart. The curries tested great, pulao delicious and a tamarind chatny (relish) just out of the world. I was in a festive mood and allowed myself the luxury to slip, just this once.

After dinner the girls pressed me to do something amusing for them. Now, it was my time to panic. I had always looked good in the audience and rarely on stage. I was still haunted by the memory of the mishap that happened decades ago during my boyhood when I was sent on stage to recite a poem called *Mary's little lamb*. I had spent days memorizing it and practicing before all the mirrors that I had access to and yet when I found myself standing on the podium looking back at an audience of several hundred people, I froze. Eventually I had to be yanked out of the stage leaving the whole audience cackling. Since then I had never returned on the stage. Trina begged but I skirted out of it. Kids are equally nice and cruel; they never forget the embarrassing things. I wasn't about to take another risk at this point of my life.

Hashem bhai saved me from this jeopardy. He pulled out a collection of poem by the famous Bengali writer 'Nazrul Islam' and recited several poems. He wasn't very good at it but that didn't seem to discourage him by any means.

Julekha bhabi, in her attempt to make our experience even better, went on to make a huge homemade cake. Unfortunately the oven did not fully cooperate and the thing didn't turn out very well. The kids were eagerly waiting for the cake and they seemed to get turned off by this disappointment. Hashem bhai's big smile and the commitment to replace the 'worthless' oven did very little to change the gloominess of the young faces.

Pushpa looked particularly depressed. "There are so many nice cakes in the stores!" She said almost mournfully. "We never buy those. Since we came to Canada we have become so poor!"

Her words dropped like a bomb. Shili and I were both caught unprepared for such turn of event. Poverty had never been an unusual event in any of our lives. Born and raised in a poor country like Bangladesh one must endure the constant reminder of poverty in practically every moment of the day – on the streets, in the slums, in the villages or cities equally. It was never something to despise. However, when a kid so dear to us spells it out then the impact becomes something totally different. Not knowing what I could do to help the situation I proposed to quickly get a cake from the nearby store to which both Hashem bhai and Julekha bhabi objected vehemently. We learned that in Pushpa's real birthday a cake worth 70 dollars were purchased from a reputed store. Today Julekha bhabi had tried a self made cake only because her cakes always turned out very good, better than the store-made ones. For some unknown reason the thing didn't turn out right this time – could be the oven, could be the dough. She scolded Pushpa with silent eyes.

Pushpa looked at her father for some support in this dire situation.

Hashem bhai loved his daughters with his life. "She didn't say anything wrong." He lightly said. "When we lived in Malaysia we had a big house, company car and even a driver. Since we came here we do not even have a car. The girls can't go anywhere. My dear Pushpa, did I put it right?"

Pushpa nodded half heartedly.

"Dad used to make so much money in Malaysia." Trina added. "We bought all kind of stuff."

"Why did you decide to come here Hashem bhai?" I inquired.

Hashem bhai laughed meaninglessly. "For the kids, of course. The job was good but the schools weren't. Most were in Malay – a local dialect. I wanted the girls get an education in English. Everything we do is

for the kids, isn't it? However, I am thinking of going back again. I might still find another job there, if I try. What do you say sweet hearts, do you want to go back there?"
He looked at his daughters for support.

"No-o-o," was the combined response.

Now it was my turn to be surprised. "Why not?"

"Schools here are so much better." Trina and Puspha responded in harmony.

This came with an air of relief to me. The temporary hardship could not shatter the happiness that these kids found in other areas.

"We all are in the same boat." Niaz said. "My family also complains about many things but we must look at the future. By the grace of Allah my girl is getting a good education, someday she will be a successful professional."

Soon we found ourselves engaged into an in depth discussion about the pros and cons of immigration. The kids went on to get busy with their own set of games.

Women gathered back in the bedroom and discussed whatever they discuss – possibly kids, husbands, saris and jewellery.

When the offer for a second round of coffee came from Julekha bhabi our party had to break. It was already evening and Muhabbot had to go to the store. Niaz also had nightshift. Clearly he wasn't crazy about his current job but this was better than most other choices available. Before leaving he smiled weakly before saying, "There were many problems back home too. I had to resort to corruption because I had no other choice. But moneywise things were good. "

"How many times did I tell you not to come?" Nazma snapped from behind her burqa. "Never listens to me. How about now? Grass on the other side is always greener."

Hashem bhai chuckled, clearly finding it very amusing. "You are right, bhabi. What a nice way to put it! I love it."

Niaz shrugged. "So I jumped out of a frying pan into the fire, what's the difference?"

Once all the others left it was our turn to make the move. We hugged and kissed the three girls, promised to visit them again very soon and started back our drive home. Deep inside both of us must have had felt a little pity but at the same time we also knew someday these girls would become very successful and would surely be looking back at these struggling days with affectionate memories which was sure to enhance the joy of their success by manifold.

The Watermelon Saga

This happened a few years back. I had just gone through a major change in my life. To be more specific - after getting into trouble with my pervious boss, the assistant boss, the semi boss and the boss's boss I was left with no other option but to move on. Fortunately I was quick to find another engagement. I was greatly relieved being able to move out of the hot lava.

The new job was in downtown Toronto, same as the previous one, in fact in the same area. I continued to commute using the bus - subway combination, something that worked well for me as I lived in the suburb.

My office was on the eighteenth floor of a building that sprawled over a large area with its ground floor packed with all kind of stores – from fast food to shoe repair. Often I ventured down during lunch break and walked around the store lined corridors that connected to the labyrinth of Toronto's underground walkways. Particularly fond of the grocery stores I liked to watch the neatly arranged fruits in nice piles – apples, pears, oranges etc. Sometimes if I saw good discounts I even bought some and carried home after work.

One day I had walked into a grocery store during my routine stroll when I noticed a bunch of watermelons were piled up inside a wooden crate – nice, round, shiny.

I was instantly drawn. Pushing past a group of Chinese elderly folks who were crowding the watermelons I made my way near the crate, picked a round one up and was about to depart when I was rudely stopped by one of the old men. He shook a pointer right on my nose aggressively and spoke in mixed Chinese and English which if translated would mean something like, "What kind of idiot are you, man? Don't you have any knowledge about watermelon? This is a sure dud. Put it back, right now."

Alarmed I quickly put it back. Looking at their wide grins I knew I was about to do something really stupid. "Which one is good?' I innocently asked.

"Which country did you come from, you idiot?" The pointer had returned. "How can you not tell a good melon from a bad one? Watch me. "

The offended old man picked up a watermelon from the crater, carefully slapped on its midsection and listened to the resulting sound keenly. After a second and third slap the useless melon was returned to the pile and a new one was picked. This went on for a while, with the elderly men engaged into noisy consultation after each sampling. Finally, after at least a dozen watermelons, the group unilaterally agreed on one and handed it over to me. Thankful I paid six ninety nine and carried it back to my office with the plan to take it with me on my way home. I knew the sight of a whole watermelon in a public transportation could tickle the sense of humour in some people but I was ready to take the risk.

On my way home I met Azam bhai, a good friend of mine who worked for another company hosted in the same building. We both shared a keen interest in fishing. Looking at the watermelon resting on my arms he broke into roaring laughter. "What is going on here brother? Dressed in office cloths but carrying a watermelon! What were you thinking? Do you have any idea what all these people are thinking about you? Shame! Shame! Ha...ha...ha..."

I quickly looked around and inevitably caught several people smirking at me; especially noticing an attractive woman staring at the melon in a way that could be perceived as *awe stricken,* my heart just sunk. "I know. It was a stupid idea. I just couldn't control myself. It looked so good!"

Azam bhai was resourceful. He had solutions for everything. He religiously brought a backpack to work. All that ever came inside it was a small lunch box. He quickly took it off from his back. "Put the melon inside this. It is quite strong. It can hold it."

I was relieved. The watermelon fit into his oversize backpack quite nicely. I carried the bag on my hand for a while but eventually as my hands started to hurt from all the weight I hung it on my back. We got up in the train in King Station and stepped out in Bloor Station. We had to switch train here. This junction is relatively big and always crowded especially in the evenings as the office-goers return home.

The first thing that I noticed after stepping out of the train was the presence of police officers. Just a few days back there was a bomb blast in London subway. In Toronto people were more or less apprehensive as well. Canada had been very cautious about its role in the world politics but yet people with agitated minds were not particularly known to be rational. I was aware of the fact that many subway stations, particularly the larger ones, were being guarded by armed police. I had seen a few officers from a distance on my way back and forth to the office but hadn't paid much attention. However, standing several yards into the platform and facing a group of four armed officers standing right before me I had little choice but to do just that. Looking at their tense body language and over cautious posture I was instantly alarmed. The grainy image of a young man in a backpack picked up in the video cameras in London who were later found to be one of the terrorists flashed through my eyes. No wonder the backpack on my back with the watermelon inside looked suspicious. Azam bhai must have realized the mistake just about the same time. He whispered under his breath, "We are dead! Don't even think of moving. One stupid move and they are going to shoot."

Before I had a chance to respond him the police officers surrounded me in a half circle, keeping considerable distance. The big white cop who stood facing me tried to look tough and brave despite his visibly trembling fingers on the butt of his gun as he commanded, "Stop! Don't move. Not another step. Raise your hands."

I shrugged with a broad smile. 'No, no, no, it's not what you are thinking."

Azam bhai muttered," Are you nuts? Why are you talking? Just raise your hands exactly the same way I have – all the way up."

I ignored his warning and attempted to clear up this ludicrous mix-up. However, before I could even open my mouth all four officers joined forces and barked," Raise your hands. Now! Don't move!"

What a travesty! There must had been several

thousand people passing through the station who all froze, instantly identified the source of trouble and were undoubtedly ogling at my backpack. Totally freaked out I wondered whether I should be howling or roar into laughter. Me? A terrorist? Just the mere mention of them gave me goose bumps! Unsure what would be safe I instinctively followed Azam bhai and raised both my hands up, way up. "Officers, you are mistaking..." I started, still hopeful of a peaceful ending.

"Take it easy! T-a-k-e it e-a-s-y!" The short black officer who possibly also had some Indian heritage urged. "There is no need for such acts here. This is Canada. It is a peaceful country. "

I smiled with my cutest impression. "Water-melon! Just a watermelon!" I said.

Not sure if there was something in my voice or the word *watermelon* had any hidden meaning because at this point all four officers had drawn their guns. My heart rate spiked to something not experienced ever be-fore. Azam bhai whimpered, "Look how much trouble you put me in. I just want to see the faces of my children for one last time."

He spoke in Bangla, our mother tongue. A bad choice indeed as the foreign tongue worked only to ex-acerbate the suspicion of the officers, two of whom - the younger ones — had their legs visibly trembling now as they did their best to maintain a tough face. The cumula-tive restlessness that seemed to have a grip on the law officers got me quite worried at this point. I could feel a ribbon of coldness slithering up my vertebrae. My legs started to feel slightly lighter, in preparation to submit to uncontrolled shaking. Consumed by the turn of events I only hoped those two young cops didn't get into a shooting feat. I gulped in the stupid smile that had apparently worked in so many other situations and started to explain the watermelon saga as calmly as possible but who was listening? Well, if not the officers the crowd definitely was.   Not sure exactly what choice of word had triggered it but they had started to disburse at a rate faster than light – of course away from the watermelon and poor me and Azam bhai. The stampede and the resulting chaos worked a magic into the mind of the pale skin officer who suddenly found his lost wisdom and was able to keep his voice steady as he shouted, "Put your backpack down on the ground."

Fearful but happy in a way believing that finally the events were moving in the right direction my hopes rose. If I could just take that stupid backpack off my back and showed these brave hearts the offending stupid watermelon everything could just get back to normalcy and life could go on. Not so fast. As soon as I touched the backpack four guns pointed at me. "Slowly! Very slowly!" Came thundering warnings. I did as asked, to the letter. Very slowly I placed the backpack in front of my foot. My poor watermelon!

"Move back, very slowly. No tricks." Shouted the Black officer.

Tricks! If I lived through this ordeal I would donate money to the poor as a gesture of gratitude to the Almighty or whoever, I pledged. We, Azam bhai and I, obediently took a few steps back. Guns still drawn but the officers looked slightly relaxed, now that the suspicious package was on the floor and the suspects away from it. Attempting to snap up this opportunity to clear the air for a second time I quickly said, "There's just a watermelon in the bag. I bought from the grocery store near my office and taking it home. It is not a bomb or anything like that."

Using the 'b' word turned out to be a mistake of grand proportion as it instantly pushed the officers back to the defensive mode.

"Do not move! Do not move!" Shouted the officers, together.

Move? Us? We could be guilty of stupidity but definitely not bravery. Not sure whether it was caused by the trembling ground as the passengers continued to rush out of the platform or by the thundering screaming the backpack that was resting on the concrete quite peacefully suddenly started to roll toward the train line, which was located five to six feet below the platform. A fall from the platform would be a sure crashing end for the watermelon - I realized.

I politely said, "Can I get it? It's going to burst."

Burst! I meant break. What a horrible choice of word, particularly at a time like that.

The officers dived on the platform. "Do not move. Everybody on the ground. Bomb! Bomb!" They went in a screaming frenzy. Naturally.

Before my helpless eyes the watermelon rolled down the platform to the ground below and shuttered into many pieces, shooting out of the backpack. A quick glance at it and I was taken by a maddening anger. The Chinese elderly men made no mistake in picking the right melon. The deep red juicy core of the unfortunate fruit clearly displayed the promise to be ridiculously delicious. I glared at the officers in my vein attempt to burn them to ashes. Relieved and relaxed now that the truth had been revealed the officers rose to their feet brushing off the darts of their elegant dresses while also managing to issue shy, apologetic smiles.

I snatched this moment to exhaust. "I told you, didn't I? Why wouldn't you guys even listen to me? Now fix my melon. Put it together, please."

Azam bhai looked at me with exploding eyes. "What are you talking about, bro?" He whispered in our mother tongue. "Forget about the watermelon. Let's get the hell out of here."

I must have been possessed because I totally ignored him and repeated my demand perhaps with a slightly raised voice. "Please put my melon together, now."

The Caucasian officer looked at me helplessly. "How do you put a broken melon together?"

I wasn't ready to get discouraged by such technicallty just yet. "If you didn't know how to put it together then why did you let it break?"

The officers looked at each other – confused, unsure. Opportunity to grill not one, not two but a group of four police officers in public wasn't something that comes too often. Determined to squeeze the last bit of satisfaction out of it I exerted some more strong words before making my departure, obviously followed by Azam bhai who patted on my back with a big grin on his face the moment we got out of their sight.

"Well done, bro! Consider what happened to Iraq. America and their allies destroyed that beautiful country just like that watermelon. For what? To get rid of Saddam? Wasn't Saddam their agent? Why won't the terrorists bomb London? Do you expect them to bomb on my head? Useless Blair. Didn't I tell him not to attack Iraq? Think about all the people who are getting killed their everyday. Good that you said a few strong words. Put Iraq together!"

"Can you put aside all these Iraq, London stuff?" I bitterly said. "My six ninety nine just went down the drain and you are more worried about people thousands of miles away."

Azam bhai looked very hurt. "Shame on you, bro. Thousands of people died and still dying and you are lamenting about a stupid watermelon?'

When upset I tend to lose my mind completely. "I don't need to listen to such big words." I was rather annoyed. "In your whole life you have been blowing storms in a coffee cup. Have the world change?"

Trembling in anger he quickly took out seven dollars from his pocket and forced it into my hand. "Fine, take the money then, the whole seven dollars. But next time choose your words more carefully. And don't even think of calling me to go for fishing with you ever again."

While I didn't really agree with him on the matter of Iraq the concluding statement about fishing got my attention. Fishing buddies are not easy to come, not in my circle of friends. That very evening I gave him a visit at his house, returned his money and apologized for my thoughtless comments. In return he agreed to come with me for a fishing venture the coming weekend.

Porata! Oh Dear Porata!

Since I left my home country many years ago among many things what I miss the most is the handmade porata (fried flat bread). I can't vouch for others but the mornings when I woke up to see mom preparing poratas my day turned brighter. Porata with oil soaked shredded fried potatoes — I can still taste the deliciousness of that combination.

As I travelled away from home to pursue higher education in America my finances had often dwindled to the point when even buying the cheapest bread became a challenge, not to even mention about the delicacies. However, during those tough years I found a roommate who brought back some life into my dinner table. A small, middle aged Indian man Murthi was pursuing his PhD and followed a strict vegetarian diet. Soon I found out he wasn't only pretty good in mathematics but was also blessed with the heavenly skill of making delicious poratas. Oh, do I still remember those days! Who would have thought that I would travel half the world and still would be able to enjoy the oil soaked poratas with finger licking potato fries — I can feel my saliva collecting inside my mouth as I speak. Anyway, that love affair between me and the total deliciousness didn't continue very long.

Soon I was awakened in a rude realization when my clothing won't fit me anymore. Disappointed and disheartened I had to put a halt in the porata ways, indefinitely.

My university life is a matter of long past. Now, a husband and father of two, I and my family have lately moved out of a high rise Toronto apartment to a specious house in the suburb. Anybody who has lived here for even a short period of time must know how expensive it might get to have a regular housekeeper. As a result most wives end up doing chores like cooking, washing, cleaning beside other housekeeping routines unless their husbands chip in. Suffering from chronic laziness, my performance had been so poor over the years that my wife Shili had quit asking me for any help long time ago. I do have to live with a stable degree of verbal abuse, mostly the same set of speeches that evolved around my worthlessness. But since when words hurt anybody?

However, things aren't always as simple. All the stuff that you might have heard about marriage, being give and take, is true. I not helping in household affairs do no good when I beg for handmade poratas to my better half – better because she knows some things that I do not, like the secret art of making beautiful poratas. One might dare to question how difficult can it be to make some dough, separate it in little balls, roll them into flat bread and fry it in deep or little oil until lightly brown. The truth is, unless you know what you are doing you'll hit the wall right from the dough, trust me on this. I have tried several times and failed miserably. They never come up right. The other choice is to buy the packaged ones from stores. They are usually very high on oil and deemed unhealthy. All the fuss about healthy living that has started to pick up in the recent years have made into our home too.

People who live in Toronto especially in the Scarborough area knows that there are many women living in the high rise apartment buildings sell handmade poratas, dal puris (flat bread with spicy lintel mix inside) and samosas. The stuff must be refrigerated and fried in oil before serving. From our home it is a relatively long drive to pick up but we still ordered sometime, for the sake of health and palate. Most of these women live in the vicinity of the intersection of Danforth Avenue and Victoria Park Avenue - the depot for Bangladeshis. There is a reason why only the apartment dwellers are into this business. Most if not all apartment complexes in Toronto include the electricity cost within the monthly rent, as a flat rate. So, no matter how much you cook on the electric oven of yours the bill is never going to go up. In comparison the private houses have separate electric meters and the charges are based on usage. So when a renter buys a house and moves out of an apartment the usage pattern for all utilities changes instantly. The money one may make selling poratas won't be enough to pay for the extra electric bills.

It is the beginning of winter when my sister who lived in America expressed her willingness to come visit us. Their visit to our house is always a big event especially for the kids. They have one four year old son. Him and our two get along relatively well and are usually engaged into spirited plays with frequent arguments and even fights, though nothing too serious to disturb our peace. From our experiences we have noticed if they are given enough time they can usually find remedies for their own problems. Of course there is no guarantee that a few blows won't be thrown around in the process. Hence it is also a good idea to keep an eye on the progress.

Both my sister and her husband love the handmade poratas of Toronto. They have particularly asked to have them stored in plentiful well before they arrive. Porata with spicy beef curry reminds them (and us as well) of old days in Dhaka. Middle aged people must be nostalgic. On a holiday when we gorge on Khichuri (a preparation with rice and lintel) a lot of memories from old days peek through my mind as well. My better half is still little away from being in her middle ages but even she has lot of memories related to porata and sugar (there may not be too many folks from Bangladesh who haven't eaten a porata wrapped in sugar in their childhood).

Let's reign in the talk. In the event of their visit we ordered 50 poratas, some dal puris and samosas to an unfamiliar elderly woman in Toronto. My wife had tried several others who she knows but failed to get a commitment. Finally finding this lady she breathed in relief. While they are not difficult to make at home the process is time consuming, messy and requires a component of skill, hence most have them made. The women who are into this business do it for some extra income. The elderly woman's name is Aleya, I learn later. There may be something before and after but that's the only name she gives to everybody. We have never met her personally. This is the first time we ordered to her. We'll meet during pick up.

I work north of Toronto, away from all the crowd and rush of the downtown, and find it driving there is the best way to commute. Parking is available for a reasonable fee, unlike the downtown area where the parking sometimes is hard to find and often costs too much. That and of course the time to commute are two primary reason why many choose to use public transportation – subway being the popular choice with bus service as the less attractive one. I know many who frequently take naps in public transportation and they feel quite happy about the whole experience. Driving of course give no opportunity for dozing off, not without disastrous consequences, but the go-stop routine during the rush hours do provide some sort of swinging motion which is not very uncomfortable either. I have been truly enjoying the driving to work in the recent months.

On a day when I am already quite stressed pushing ridiculously heavy traffic on my way back from work Shili calls. I know right away she needs something. She never calls for nothing. The mystery reveals itself soon. She asks me to go all the way to Scarborough and pick up our order of goodies from a building on Crescent road near the intersection of Danforth Ave and Victoria Park Ave. That's where Aleya lives. On expressway 401 traffic was moving, slowly but steadily. Once I exit to the local roads things come almost to a halt. At least that's how it feels. Cursing I snap on the radio and turn the volume high, which do very little to take away my frustration. I curse Shili some, who on earth would send her husband into this mess knowingly. Somebody honks me, unduly, forcing me into a reaction where I lean on my horn for at least 10 seconds. That's what you get for honking people for nothing. Idiot!

Not sure how long have passed as I stop looking at the car clock or my watch but finally things starts to look little better. I can see the tall apartment buildings on Crescent road. This is when I realize I have completely forgotten the details like building and apartment numbers of Aleya that Shili provided me. Lately I forget a lot, things of all nature. The kids teasingly call me old and forgetful. Ironically, they are no better at it either. Often I find them teary eyed unable to find important stuff like library books, school agenda etc. with their mother eventually coming to their rescue.

I call home. It is my daughter Far who receive the phone. Since she turned four she doesn't allow anybody else to receive any call. No matter where she is and whatever she might be engaged in, she rushes and captures the phone. It is never easy to recover it from her. She isn't much into conversation. The worst part is that she gets hold of the receiver and continue with her business - whatever she has been doing before the interruption. After screaming 'Hello' three four times when I receive no response I give up and call Shili on her cell phone instead who took her sweet time before receiving. I learn my daughter is willing to talk to me but she needs to finish the feeding routine of her baby doll first. Mad in frustration I am about to say something rude but then have to reign in. She is the only one in the family who seems to genuinely care about me, unlike her mother and brother, being sarcastic.

I get the building number from Shili. She does not know the apartment number or the buzzer number. She has only spoken to Aleya only once. Aleya could not give her all the details. Shili tells me to call Aleya up and get the details. She is busy and do not have time to make the call. She disconnects. What I feel can easily be described as overwhelming rage. I need to know the buzzer number – without it getting inside the building could be quite difficult. Usually it is possible to tag along others but then there are those moments where some people would give you that suspicious look, rightfully so – *who the hell are you? Where are you planning to go?* I hate that.

I call Aleya, after fourth ring I get the answering machine and leave a message. *I have come to pick up the poratas but I can't get in. I do not have your buzzer or the apartment number. Please call at my cell phone as soon as you get this message.* Fifteen minutes passes and when nobody calls me back, quite annoyed I call Aleya again. Four rings and pops up the answering machine. Unsure about what to do – leave another message or just disconnect – a broken female voice interrupts my thought. "'I am Aleya. Who are you? Hello?"

I give her my name and explain my intention. I ask for her apartment number and buzzer number.

A few moments silence. "Son, I have no clue what is the buzzer number. It is never required. So many people are coming and going all the time, just follow them."

I let go a sigh. "What is your apartment number?"

Some more silence. "Can't remember son. Two thousand something. I came here only four months ago. How can anybody remember all these things in such a short time?"

I shrug. I have to wonder how this woman continues to do this business when she doesn't even know this very basic information. I ask her if she can come down to the lobby and hand me over the goodies.

"I can't do that. " She hesitantly responds. "I do not have any keys for the apartment. My daughter and son-in-law went to work. They won't be back in another hour or so."

I feel a slight headache progressing inside my head. How did I get myself into this? I wasted minimum one hour pushing through the traffic to get here, going back without the poratas is not an option. I try to think. Is there any other useful information I can fetch from Aleya?

"Which floor do you live in?" I finally ask.

"Didn't I say two-thousand-something? " She snapped. "Two thousand means twentieth floor – how can you not know this?"

I try to be patient. Somebody who doesn't know her apartment number is in no way to lecture. When is she going to learn that?

"Which way should I go once I am on 20th floor?" I ask.

"Turn right. I'll open the door and look for you. You'll know me right away. All my hair is gray. Come up, son. I am going to get your package ready."

She disconnects. I notice many returning office workers are entering the building in hoards. Several seniors have gathered in the lobby for an afternoon gossip. It is almost end of fall, there is clear chill in the air. Light jacket isn't doing it anymore. I follow couple of gentlemen and slip through the door with as much normalcy as I can possibly master. None of the gentlemen even look back to see me. Everyday thousands of people enter and exit these buildings. Who has time to check on others? At least that's what I believed. I am up for a rude awakening when one of the oldest ladies among the group of seniors takes a few quick and unsteady steps ahead propping against her stick and blocks my way. Damn! What is she up to?

"Where do you think you are going?" The Caucasian old lady demanded, with an extra bit of roughness in her trembling voice.

I was visibly shaken. This isn't something I was expecting. Why does she care where I am going? Who gave her the right to question me?

"Umm, up." I have to look for words.

The old lady   checks me out with her sharp eyes. "I know everybody who lives in this building. Everybody — man, woman, kids. You are an outsider. Did you think just because I grew old you can fool me? I can pick you up in the air and slam on the ground just like that..." She gestured threateningly.

Now, this is the right time for me to start to panic. If this lady continues to make too much noise others might stop to inquire, somebody may call the security, at the end everything will flow downward. Her companions group up and walk toward me, making me even further nervous. The old lady continues her lecture, "You can't just enter as you wish. Hold on, I am going to call the police. Does anybody have a phone?" She asks her companions.

There is a series of head shakes — 'no'. She looks at me. "Hand me over your phone".

I look around me. If things go too far I am ready to dash out. Let the porata go to hell. When the whole population of the world streaming through these buildings without any problem why do I have to get so unlucky to face this trouble? I stubbornly shake my head. No way (I am handing over my cell phone to her).

She narrows her eyes and examines me for a few long moments. "Think you are too smart? Okay, go ahead, I forgive you this time. However, if I see you again I am calling the cops. Remember that."

I let go a breath of relief and rush to catch the waiting elevator. It is jam packed. Office traffic meets with the army of kids who are travelling back and forth to the playground. Every button on the floor panel is lit - from two to all the way twenty. Patience and more patience. As the elevator continues its slow journey up stopping and unloading at every level, I try to take a short nap leaning against the wall at one corner of the elevator, unsuccessfully.

Once at 20th floor I follow Aleya's instruction and turn right. I continue to walk through the long corridor hoping to see Aleya peaking out. Nothing. I walk across the length of the corridor three times with no luck. I call her again. The door opens this time with Aleya peaking through it. She is about sixty. She looks older than her age but have an affectionate smile.

"Sorry for the trouble son. I rarely go out, do not know anything around here. Come inside. Nobody is home."

I step inside. A two-bedroom apartment neatly arranged - expensive sofas, large dining table, tasteful oil paints hanging from the wall. The kitchen however is a total mess. Aleya received some new orders, I learn. Our order is ready and set to go.

"I get many orders son," she smilingly say. "My

porata goes all the way to America. Everybody likes my porata. It makes me so happy. Keeps me busy too. I actually have three other deliveries this afternoon. They might show up soon."

Great! Why should I be the only one getting tormented by the crazy old lady in the lobby? I pay and is about to leave with my goodies when Aleya stops me. "Do you want to see some pictures? I have two grandchildren. So restless! Hold on for a second, I'll go and get the albums."

As I wait in the living room, out of word, Aleya hurries into one of the bedrooms to get the picture albums. I stand there, shocked, wondering how she can trust somebody who she has never met before. This city is filled with thugs!

I have to go through several albums. She has only one child – a daughter, who is a nurse by profession. Half the albums are filled with her childhood photos. I sit through it not knowing if it will be too rude to just walk away. At some point the torturous session ends and she goes to put the albums back. Several minutes later she returns and gives me this surprised look. "Who are you son? Are you waiting for something? Sorry, I forgot. I have become very forgetful. "

I sigh. I take a mental note to ask Shili to speak to Aleya's daughter. She probably has no clue how bad her mother's memory is. As I remind her about the porata she feels very embarrassed. "So sorry! I totally forgot about that. I am getting old. But my porata is very delicious. Do you want me to fry one for you? I have potato fries. The two goes together very well."

Really! Potato fries? I am torn in between. I eat

light lunches. By the time it is late afternoon my stomach usually churns in hunger. I can feel saliva rushing toward my mouth. At the end I control my urge and step out into the corridor with the load of poratas and other goodies, anxiously wondering how the traffic is going to be on my way to home. There is a short wait for the elevator, fortunately. As I walk out to the lobby I am happy to find out that the crazy lady is still posted there. Imagining the other porata pickers going through the same peril as I did, I chuckle. At my sight her eyes narrows in a deep frown, examines my goody bag and goes up a pointed finger stabbing in the air menacingly – *if I see you again...* Fat chance! I am going to walk out, climb into my car and drive off never to return. I give her a crooked smile and step outside pushing through the heavy door. The door shut down with a loud bang right behind me.

I have just opened the car door and dropped the load inside when the phone rings. It is Shili.

"There is a problem." She said.

"What problem?" I show enough terseness to discourage her from any further request. I want to return home. Show any weakness and she will find ten other things for me to do.

"Aleya called. Right after you got into the elevator. She gave you the wrong bag."

"What!" I bark.

There is a long silence at the other end. "Please go back one more time. She begged me. Would you, please?"

Annoyed I take a quick look into the lobby through the glass panels. The crazy lady is still there. There is no way I am going to face her again. She will just eat me alive this time.

"Did she give us the bigger one or the smaller one?"

"Bigger. Much bigger."

I take a long breath. It is going to sound really mean but I have no choice. I say, "Call her back and say you could not reach me." I disconnect.

We eat those porotas with great pleasure. Aleya didn't exaggerate, her porata is delicious. We have lot of words of praise for her. However, some of our friends may have heard some nasty things about me. Aleya's daughter is a close friend of one of our family friends. Later it comes to my knowledge that she has been told I am one of the meanest people on earth. I have taken advantage of a clueless woman's poor memory and stole poratas. The earth would have been a much better place to live if it wasn't for people like us.

How ridiculous! Why do I have to take all the blame!

Seven Bodies on a Dirt road

At fifty, Kamal looked older. He was small, barely five feet. His tanned skin and a mild face instantly revealed his South East Asian identity. As he walked through the bustling summer crowds in his faded jeans and half sleeve cotton tee shirt he appreciated the unusual warmth for late August. Coming from a country where the coldest nights were warmer than often chilling Canadian fall, he dreaded the winter. Immigrated to Canada twenty years ago he still struggled to cope up with the freezing northern cold. He would rather take the tropical monsoon, the scorching sun and the occasional deadly floods.

Kamal walked in exceptionally long strides for a person so small, his hands swung rhythmically beside his body, his head down in deep thoughts. He worked as a part time mechanic for a motor vehicle garage in the vicinity of his house, near the intersection of Warden and Eglinton Ave. in Scarborough. He had several part time jobs, which ranged from gas station to fast food. An experienced Mechanical Engineer, he had gone through all kinds of jobs since coming here, none had anything to do with his professional expertise. There was a time when he complained, wrote to every government offices he could possibly think of, rallied in front of parliament, posted innovative posters urging Canadians to protest and several other things that he couldn't even remember. After twenty years this had become way of life. He understood he had a choice. He could leave. He didn't. He settled down, bought a small house and raised two kids to their adulthood. His wife Mita worked in Wal-Mart, fulltime. Daughter of a judge back home it wasn't easy for her. But she learned. Everybody learns when the situation demands. Kamal knew that. Just years ago he knew nothing about cars, now he could open the damn thing up and put it back together. No problem.

Raghu Sing gave him a long look. A Punjabi, he was quite tall and had lighter complexion. A charming man for a garage owner he was liked by his employees. He looked young but Kamal suspected he was in his late forties.

"Anything bothering you, boss?" Kamal inquired.

"You are early." Raghu briefly replied in his characteristic calmness.

Kamal didn't take offense. He was known for untimely arrivals. He was a good worker when he worked and definitely was an amicable person. Raghu ignored his lack of punctuality.

"I have to leave little early today, boss" Kamal said as he punched in.

Raghu usually didn't ask too many questions unless he had to. Happy with Kamal's informal excuse he moved on to check some recent news on the computer that sat on his large desk. The mechanics were all paid by the hour.

Kamal drank a glass of tap water. On a regular day he would just move on to the garage area and drown into his work. He was known for his quietness and devotion. Today he lingered in the office longer. Raghu sensed there was something else. "What are you up to buddy?"

"Today we have that meeting." Kamal brightened up. "The one about the war crimes. I told you about it earlier."

Raghu had good memory. He nodded. Yes, he remembered. This was something Kamal had been looking forward to for months. Kamal was an active campaigner to bring the war criminals of Bangladesh to justice. In 1971, when the Eastern part of unified Pakistan fought for sovereignty and freedom a minority group betrayed the general population in the name of religious integrity and collaborated with West Pakistan. They actively assisted the enemy in seeking out and murdering the intellectuals and leaders of their own country. Later that year neighboring India had gotten involved and helped East Pakistan to defeat the invading army. That's how Bangladesh was born. Raghu, an Indian, was only in his preteen at that time but remembered some of it. Many mistakenly thought it was just another war between India and Pakistan, the two archrivals in South East Asia. Such negligence flared up Kamal like a matchstick. He had lost family in that war, several. He took everything about it damn seriously.

Raghu was careful about his choice of words.

"Oh, really!" He showed sufficient interest.

"An expatriate professor from Australia is coming as a chief guest. There will be hundreds of people. It's about time we put those murderers to justice." Kamal was uncharacteristically loud. "After all these years, the movement is finally starting to take shape. The meeting will be in a party center on Danforth Avenue. Why don't you come along, boss?"

Raghu shifted his weight to the other side of his body. For some strange reason Kamal had this impression that Raghu shared similar rage about the war criminals of 1971. He didn't. He had nothing to do with them. He carefully hid his feelings. "How can I? I got to keep the garage open. You go ahead. My blessings are with you." He chuckled just to ensure Kamal understood that he was joking about the blessings. Kamal didn't need his blessings. Not out of this garage.

Kamal nodded in agreement, poured a cup of coffee from the coffee pot placed on a small corner table. No milk no sugar, he liked his coffee black.

"We'll get them, boss." He said. "Ironically, many of those murderers are living right here. I don't understand the policies of Canadian government. Why allow these criminals to swarm this country? Aren't they supposed to do background checks?"

This question wasn't thrown directly at Raghu. It was more like a monologue. Raghu refrained from making any comments. He expected Kamal to get to work. If he had to leave early he needed to start working on his assignment.

Kamal knew that as well. He left the office with the coffee in his hand and walked into the specious garage area right beside the office. Dozens of cars sat inside for servicing. Two Caucasian mechanics greeted him and expressed their astonishment in his early arrival. Kamal smiled at them, greeted back and walked to a Nissan Altima. This was his assignment. He did some work the previous day, but there was plenty of work left. It had issues from ignition to break pads. Practically no serious maintenance was done over the years. He had spoken to the owner when she came to drop it off. An eighty something black lady who just didn't realize even a new car had to be serviced in regular intervals.

Finishing his coffee in quick successive sips he opened the hood and unmindfully poked inside. Everything needed maintenance. Cars, houses, countries, independence. Twenty years ago he had to literally flee his country, the country he lost most members of his family for. A reputed engineer in a government job, he was threatened with dire consequences for not going along with bribery schemes. He played along for a little while, just long enough to arrange his immigration to Canada.
He sighed. Life here wasn't without its own twists. He escaped the corruption, only to be dumped into embarrassment. He took it well though. Mita was strong, supporting. They walked the walk for the future of their kids – son Manju and daughter Rita. While he blocked Manju from his mind, thought of Rita filled him with pride and joy. A top student in her class she was midway through her Computer Science degree at McGill. Tears formed in his eyes. How much he wished Manju had stick to his education instead of settling with a fast food job! At twenty-four he was equipped with a high school diploma, a useless goatee and couple of unsightly earrings. His mother found them funny, Kamal didn't. He looked strange to him, foreign, someone Kamal couldn't relate

to. But yet he hardly ever objected fearing that would trigger Manju to leave home. His mother and sister loved and cared for him, whether he knew it or not. Kamal let out a deep breath. Only if Manju had gone through what he did in his teen years! Manju was like a little kid, yet to be nurtured to his full potential.

As his hands and eyes coordinated on the subtle elements of the car, his mind somehow found a way to drift back in time. The war had started months ago, enemies pushed through villages after villages in search for the freedom fighters, many of whom were trained in bordering India and returned to join the overall resistance against the West Pakistan's aggression deep into its neglected Eastern part. Kamal's family had several fighters including his dad, two older brothers, one uncle and one cousin brother. His father Ajam, a regional commander of the resistance was idolized by young fighters. He had foresight, coolness and pragmatism. Even when the pro-Pakistani religious zealots joined forces with the ruthless enemy and hindered the progress of the freedom fighters with their betrayal and brutality, he still held high hope and morality. Kamal, a fourteen year old, would have done anything to be allowed to fight. Every time he held one of the rifles his family fighters had, this blazing anger rushed through his veins, his fingers tightened around the trigger, lips hardened. He was ready to kill the hyenas, the beasts that left trails of burned villages with rotting corpses of commoners and sexually violated women – young or old. Ajam dismissed his eagerness citing his tender age. He was told to wait. His time would come.

He remembered the day as if it was yesterday. . It was early November, a Friday. The village market was buzzing with people wearing second hand sweaters and Indian shawls. The mild winter was refreshing after intense summer. Just days ago the local fighters had ambushed a fleet of enemy soldiers in a nearby village and killed majority of them. Everybody knew the enemy would come looking for the fighters. Ajam and his team moved out of their houses and took shelter in an underground cellar below the local mosque, something that they had secretly built. The enemy was Muslim in religion and wasn't expected to intrude a mosque without any solid information.

The soldiers came around noon. The buzzing subsided magically as the fleet of army vehicles carefully approached the crowded market. Many had left in hurry, others hid inside shops and the rest froze in their respective positions. There was no telling what was ensuing. Kamal went to get some cooking oil for his mother. Almost reflexively he slipped behind a nearby bush, his curious eyes peeking through the dense branches. The soldiers forced seven fighters on the ground from an army truck, blindfolded, unrecognizable in blood, broken bones and torn flesh. They were then shoved to the middle of the dirt road; lined up in a row and thrown on the dirt, face down.

Time stopped for Kamal. He looked at the determined faces of the fighters - his father, uncle, brothers and two other young men. Somebody had betrayed. The enemy was tipped off. He knew it. Everybody did. Nobody outside this village was supposed to know where the fighters were hiding.

Punched out, Kamal waited at the front of the garage. Manju was supposed to drop him at the meeting venue. The family had no car. Manju sometimes borrowed an old vehicle form one of his close friends. Kamal usually commuted using TTC - the bus and train combo. Today, considering the time constraint he had asked Manju for a ride.

The meeting would start at six. He had only twenty minutes in hand. Manju didn't show up. He wasn't surprised. He wondered how little he expected from his son, once a wonderful little boy with keen interest in being a spell bee champion.

Raghu, knowing how important the meeting was, offered him a ride. Danforth Avenue was only a short distance away. His nephew could handle the shop until he returned. When they reached the venue it was ten past six. Fortunately the meeting hadn't started yet. It was a relief. Kamal didn't want to miss any part of it. This meeting was the effort of a whole lot of people who had been working on this for years with no outcome, as the political parties back home joined hands with the traitors to secure majority in the national assembly. Damn politicians!

The meeting started amid a large gathering in the medium sized auditorium. As the speakers after speakers spoke about the undeniable brutalities, the deaths, the massacres and the deadly betrayals Kamal did something that he hadn't done for very long time – he wept. Tears rolled down his cheeks. He wasn't ashamed anymore.

The passing years couldn't smudge the vividness of the trauma that he bore deep inside. That dirt road! He came in this meeting with lot of anger but all he could do was shed tears.

What happened next was unthinkable. During the speech of the guest speaker a group of unruly youth invaded the center and went on a rampage. Instantly the place became a battleground as the crowd fought back. Thrown into total confusion Kamal didn't even know how he was shoved out of the center on the street. Punched and kicked he desperately crawled behind a dumpster. A swarm of cops came rushing. Chases and beatings were followed by several arrests. Stores closed, pedestrians gone, the place looked deserted.

Kamal, blood thickening on his face, couldn't collect the courage to step out. Sitting in a coiled up position his mind went blank. Who would think here in Toronto such thing could happen? The current government back home had collaborated with the traitors. The supporters of government staged the trouble. He knew for sure. Damn politics! It eats up people's conscience.

"Dad!"

Startled, Kamal looked back to find Manju.

"Sorry dad," Manju said, "I forgot about your meeting. I came to pick you up after the meeting. Come on."

Manju towered over him, had strong, muscular hands. He helped Kamal to the passenger sit and wiped the blood off his face. "Just a minor cut. You'll be okay." He comforted.

On the drive back home silence prevailed, as always.

"Dad, it's been thirty six years!" Manju broke the silence, casually.

"So what?" Growled Kamal. "They slaughtered them, right in front of my eyes. They kicked the heads like worthless sack of bones. They drove over the dead bodies. They were my family, for God's sake! Don't you understand?"

Manju gave him a sympathetic look. He understood more than he expressed. Silenced followed.
Pulling the car in the narrow driveway of their house, he took a moment before breaking the news. "I am going back to college, dad. This fall."

Kamal looked briskly at him before climbing out of the car. He felt feverish and needed to collapse on a bed. Nevertheless, a grain of hope sparkled deep inside him. Not all was bad today.

Good Morning Toronto

Rocking through the misty sea my dream boat had just arrived to the majestic kingdom when the monstrous witch screamed me out of my sweet sleep into the unusually harsh reality of daybreak. Terrified that the noise would interrupt the Queen and four year old prince, I sprung out mightily and slapped it shut. Quarter to eight. Summer sun seemed to beam from somewhere in the mid sky. When bedtime is usually well past midnight this feels like dawn. While forcing the glued eye lashes to open, I felt my way to the washroom. Another quickie while I release. Not used to wetting my body in the mornings, I brushed in a vain attempt to glitter my sparsely lined naturally yellow teeth, managed to put myself into a pair of trousers and a shirt, next the feet wrapped in socks and shoes, I grabbed my cheap black bag and stumbled out of our apartment to the corridor.

A heavy voice startled me. I remembered the middle aged gentleman. He lived just a few apartments away. He stayed with his son. He came not very long ago. Often I find him pacing across the long corridor. Every time we met he greeted me enthusiastically. I assumed he had nobody to talk to. His son and daughter in law both worked. They left pretty early to beat the traffic.

Though I didn't consider myself much of a social person under best condition I could hold up a conversation for a little while but this wasn't the moment. Especially in the morning I hated to talk. I tried to reward him with my best smile and slip through but that wasn't to be. He grabbed me by the soldier. I had to stop.

"Went to the doctor yesterday. Low blood pressure. He told me not to worry. Ha…ha…ha… Benefits of walking. What did I tell you?"

His English was poor. He spoke mostly in Hindi. I understand quite a bit but can't speak at all. Yet in situation like this I somehow manage. I mumbled something ineligible and stepped away. I worked downtown Toronto. I commuted in public transportation. The trip was never less than one and half hour. I could drive to work but considering the packed roads during the office hours it would probably take even longer. I had little patience for traffic. And there was rocketing parking costs in the city. The additional car insurance for driving to work added salt to the wound. Public transportation worked perfectly for me. They called it TTC. Anyway, Time was in essence. There was no time to indulge this gentleman.

My journey consisted of a bus trip followed by three different trains. Today I noticed there was a long line for the bus. Everyday was different. No amount of observation helped me come up with a pattern that worked on regular basis. As the bus arrived the crowd rushed in. Oh well, being polite was good thing but a nudge here and a shove there to occupy an empty seat wasn't totally out of question. Inside the bus was packed with people. Black and white, pink and brown. Right ahead me stood a towering black man with his shaved head pushing the roof. Under his arms sat a guitar. Looking around I saw people of various races, sizes and ages gathered in this small space, a true junction. I felt good. Such observation of internationality was bound to awake the versatile humanity in anybody. I felt proud to be part of this community.

Our bus pushed through the heavy stop-and-go rush hour traffic. Next station. More people; pushed closer; hot; sweating. Even in this crowd Salim didn't fail to see me. He pushed through the crowd to my side.

"How'z going brother? Going to office, huh? You did well. Look at me? I am a complete failure."

Salim came from Dhaka, the capital of Bangladesh. He held a high position in a computer section of an established company. He was young. I didn't know what had motivated him to come all the way to Canada. But since he came here his luck didn't offer much. He worked in a store in Scarborough center. It was hard not to feel guilty. I had immigrated long ago and went through long and painful times to get where I was, which was not that far, but I didn't want to tell that to this young intelligent man.

Salim bitterly said, "Brother, you didn't do anything for me."

I wish I could explain to him how limited my ability was. We climb out of the bus at the same station. Our ways departed. I hurried up on the stairs to catch the RT. This train would carry me to Kennedy station from where I would be able to catch the underground train – the subway.

Once in Kennedy I bolted down the stairs to catch the next train. Hoping inside the train right before the doors closed I felt my lips cracking into a happy smile. Seconds later the train left the brightly lit station and rushed into the dark tunnel. As I gazed inside the well lit compartment I noticed calm and patient office goers – well dressed, well mannered! Merging into the crowd I desperately looked for a handle to stabilize myself. The drivers often applied brakes pretty hard, catching inattentive people into sudden stumble. After accidentally crashing into several attractive women I had to be careful about it. I didn't want anybody to get wrong ideas.

Very often I ran into acquaintances in the subway trains. One of the cons of changing work too often was that you knew a lot of people but very few actually became close friends. I worked as a IT contractor. A handful of my contracts went beyond a year. Anyway, bad luck hit me today. I ran into Rajan. He was younger than me, had immigrated to Canada long ago, was street smart. His only problem was he asked the darn questions. Today he abruptly asked, "how much do you make?"

I turned deaf. You don't ask the age of a woman and the salary of a man – even the most gullible person knew that, not Rajan. It reminded me of an incident that happened at home a few days back. One morning my four year old son got very excited and frantically called me. I ran fearing some sort of emergency. At my sight the boy gloriously declared, "Dad, I have two balls. How many do you got?"

Rajan wasn't to be discouraged. He repeated his question as I put up a blank face. Helpless I mumbled something and moved on closer to the door. My station was next. I would have to take yet another train to my work. Run! Run! I stumbled down the stairs. As I struggled to regain my balance I heard somebody playing guitar. A man sung in deep, passionate voice. He was a familiar face around here, one of many musician panhandlers. Some played instruments, some sung, seldom they care dabout the quality. If the pedestrians liked the acts they threw in changes. Unfortunately I was one of those frugals who wasn't much into giving handouts, with or without music. Regardless I had a lot of respect for these street musicians.

Another short trip brought me to a station with a majestic name – King station. I rushed out of the train, followed the crowd up the narrow stairs into the sunlit streets as streams of sweat tingled me under my shirt. One good thing about all that running around was that it sort of worked as an alternative of planned work outs.

I worked in one of the buildings of Toronto Dominion Center located in the downtown. This was literally a hub for financial activities. Multistoried office buildings belonging to several of the major banks like Scotiabank, TD bank, CIBC and Bank of Montreal surrounded the vicinity. Swarms of well dressed people, man and women, marched busily in and out of the behemoths. And yet I knew so many others were left behind, especially the new immigrants, lacking neither in education not in experience they were left behind their only crime appeared to be not having any local experience. They were forced into odd jobs – working in the shops, stores, restaurants for a humble living. I couldn't help feeling guilty.

Younge street was the magic wand of Toronto. I kept walking past a series of high rise office buildings. At my work a lonely desk and a chair waited for me. Nearby

CN tower stood boldly spearing through the air into the blue sky. A mesmerizing view! Suddenly a rugged hat, upside down, popped up right in front of my face. Startled I took a step back but quickly realized it was just another homeless asking for hand outs. Yet another guy who made the streets his home. I had seen several just in this small area. Mostly whites some had companion dogs, large furry ones. A lonely homeless man with a large quiet dog – there could be a touch of poetic beauty in this scenario but it was far more heart breaking. I heard government in this country tried many ways to help the homeless, very little progress was being made, the proof of that was so evident everywhere. I never felt comfortable in giving away handouts. I had seen how such demeaning tradition eventually turned into a social disease back in my native country. The fear of watching similar corrosion in this society brought terrible feelings.

As I approached my workplace, a multistoried building, I saw another young homeless man lying flat on the sidewalk on a piece of rug enjoying the morning sun. The bright rays touched him gently. With his eyes closed and a smile holding static between his lips, he seemed to have learned the trick to ignore the restive world allowing it to pass by unnoticed. He had no conventional home, so the world became his only home. I felt a sudden rush of rebeliousness, an uncontrollable urge to jump out of my office dress and lie down next to him, right on the sidewalk. Wouldn't it be great, at least for once, to get out of my shell and morph into an entity devoid of any worldly belongings!

I quickly went past the man as always and walked into the specious lobby. A short wait for the elevator. My office was on the 25th floor. Well secured. The magical card called a badge did its magic and the doors opened up for the majesty, the waiting desk and the chair silently welcomed me. Staring at the computer monitor for a few brief moments I was suddenly flooded with a feeling of abomination. This work, this office, this life everything felt like a burden, something that I carried diligently day after day, month after month, year after year. As a young boy I had so many plans, so many dreams. All that had come to an end, at some point of my journey, little I realized. A voice inside my mind screamed out announcing the worhlessness of my life!

At my right sat Sasa from Russia. At my left was Murali from India. Opposite to him sat Beth from China. After an argument with the manger she wrote a long two page letter filled with objectionable statements about the manager and then mistakenly sent it to the manager. Once she realized her mistake a second email was sent quickly with the request to ignore the previous email. That issue didn't just go away for her, not before causing lot of administrative problems.

I had to get down to work, willing or not. I didn't have the luxury to hop into twisted adventures. I had a family and reminiscent of dreams. I needed to keep going, after all in this new land I was one of the fortuantes with a cushioned revolving chair at work and a company laptop. But somewhere deep inside me the rebel continued to knock its head on a cold wall of normalcy.

At 11 Am came the phone call from the prince. "Happy office dad!"

The Forbidden View

Lately, life hadn't been fair to him. He had this simple expectation of a peaceful and comfortable retirement life with his loving family but things couldn't have gone any worse. His fate had conspired on him. It concocted an all-proof plan to cheat on him. Lonely and miserable, he felt his final days were approaching him quickly disregarding his reluctance to call it an end. An immense shadow of anger had settled deep inside him over the years like a persistent headless ghost. He didn't want to quit with so much fire within. At dusk as the last rays of the sun disappeared, he felt a sudden urge of desire. There was so much he wanted, there was so much he needed.

Lately, his thoughts were occupied with his x-wife. Thirty years ago on a dreamy, summer night they had their vows made in a traditional Bangladeshi marriage ceremony followed by the cherished wedding night, the first time together. The beautiful and shy nineteen-year bride, younger by a whopping sixteen years, shook his world to the core. She sat quietly on the rosy bed clad in red Benaroshi – a beautiful wedding sari, too shy to even look up at her groom, while he anchored at the far end of the bed, equally shy but yet curious enough to gawk at her. Oh, those large dark doe eyes on a sharp little face! Who knew a marriage among unknown could generate such wonderful emotions! Just the thought of growing old with that angelic woman felt so overwhelming. Sitting there silently he fought hard to find something nice to say, something that they would recall years later fondly, smilingly. Time passed, his words unfound, mouth dry. Nervous wreck, he gulped a glass of water, stealthily. This prompted an instant giggle by the bride. He should have felt embarrassed but he didn't. The melody of that first laughter had him awed. He watched and listened. In his heart he felt like Alexander the Great, a worrier, a conqueror. Just to hear that magical sound of the giggle he gulped another glass of water.

Later, still no words spoken he had turned the lights off to facilitate a good night's sleep. Lying down far from his bride, at a distant corner of the incredibly wide bed, he cursed himself for all his inabilities. He had waited for this night for so long, through painful days of celibacy – a common practice in his society, and when finally it came, he felt scared, anxious and unprepared. He listened the rhythmic breathing of the bride, yards away, yet felt so worm and soft. The night grew older and quieter. The clouds overshadowed the stars and finally gave up into a sudden convulsion of rain bringing in some relief to the wrath of blazing tropical heat. The open windows invited the spattered raindrops accompanied by the cool breeze. The bed was getting soaked, the pillows wet.

"It's getting wet." Muttered the bride; almost in a monologue.

"Should I close the windows?" He asked, happy to finally find an excuse to say anything useful.

"Shouldn't we?" Came a soft reply.

He was off in a jiffy. The bride giggled once again. Oh, the fluid, melodious and the magical sound!

"Why do you laugh?" He could collect enough courage to say.

"I don't know." A playful answer. His silence was interrupted shortly. "Don't you want to kiss me?" A sensuous voice whispered.

He had this intense urge to embrace her petite, beautiful body in his strong arms and rock it with passionate kisses. In reality his body went ice cold. He couldn't even move a finger.

The bride chuckled. A touch of empathy and affection was clearly detectable. Her fear and anxiety of an arrange marriage disappeared quickly. The intimacy that ensued became the beginning of a wonderful life together.

After two decades of happy, conjugal life that sweet and supportive woman, mother of their only child, their daughter, left him for a younger man, a man she briefly once described as smart, lively and enthusiastic. He had known him for years and liked him in a way. Not for once he had suspected the strange romance that bloomed so secretly yet so openly, right before his eyes. What more she wanted? He had given her everything - love, wealth, child and honor. What else might have driven her to the unknown? He didn't have the answer. He never really looked for it. Unfathomable shame and anger filled him, leaded him to the darker side.

Lately, he thought a lot about his daughter, their only child. When she was only six he had noticed an unusual calmness in her, an abnormal level of self-consciousness. She used to get annoyed at the company of her parents, avoided being the subject of unending attention. When faced with affection she gave this cold stare that would make anybody uncomfortable. Her strong personality made it impossible to deal with her on any account. Anything that she disapproved had to be gone or most annoying circumstances would be in the offing. Cigarette was one such unfavorable object to her. If he had ever lighted one in front of her she would look with abomination.

"Dad, don't smoke. I hate it."

"Just one, sweetheart."

"No, not a single one."

"I am cutting back, you know. Long time habit, not so easy to quit. " He reasoned.

"Spare me that pathetic monologue."

Such unusual rudeness had equally surprised and hurt him, forced him to watch every minor things he did or said at her presence. Many sleepless nights passed worrying about her.

During her college years she stayed home for a little while, in the beginning. Despite all the differences he had always enjoyed her company. A child was a child, through disrespect and sardonic times. Nevertheless, one day she announced coldly that she was moving to a residential hall.

"Why?" Shocked, he asked.

"I hate to stay here." The answer was abrupt, precise. "I hate everything here. You, mom, this big house - everything."

He was hurt deep inside. For long eighteen years

he had given her unconditional love. The usual coldness he could take, even the occasional rudeness but this went far beyond. He and his wife had known her well by then. None objected.

The girl didn't have a great time in the residential hall. He received frequent letters from the authorities – "Your daughter is confused about her sexuality. Talk to her. "

In a conservative Muslim society homosexuality had no chance. Confused and clueless, he rushed to see her, repeatedly. She wouldn't see him. Eventually she left the residential hall and later the college. She didn't come home. Not then, not ever. Soon after, his dearest wife had followed. There was no 'Dear John' letter, no discussions, no phone calls. He received papers for divorce, few days later. That was it.

He had loved these two women so dearly but neither he understood them nor could become anything more than a stranger. Often he felt his misfortune had started right at birth when her mother had died in the hand of a village mid-wife who handled the normal cases perfectly well but were clueless with exceptions. A young wife's live was exchanged for the baby boy, the light of the family. The guilt that he carried all his life had never faded. Every time life took a low punch at him he absorbed quietly. It was payback time.

Lately, he reminisced his early teen years. During that time of unusual and often uncomfortable physical changes came along sudden rush of strange but very overpowering feelings. Alone in a room, walking fully naked and observing the novelty of a sudden hardness would fill him with intense pleasure and satisfaction! One unfortunate day, one of his uncles accidentally walked on him. The need for privacy for a child was not a requirement. The uncle, seeing what he saw, had created maximum commotion.

"What's wrong with you? Why are you going around naked? Are you turning into a jungle boy or something? Do we now have to release you in a forest?" His sarcasm had no bound.

Ashamed and confused he zoomed out of the house and stayed hiding until very late. Uncle had a blast at his cost. Everybody in his joint family had known every tiny details of that encounter. Soon, he became the center of gossip for every female in the house. His sightings invariably met with chuckles, giggles and whispered remarks. For months he moved through the house stealthily.

The next spring one of his aunts, a young wife at her early twenties came to visit them after several years. Since the wedding few years ago her beauty had become a popular topic of talk in the surrounding villages. With her unusual milky white complexion, waist long dark black hair and the big clear dark eyes she looked stunning, a portrait of a divine beauty. It was love at first sight. No courage to talk, he followed her around secretly. Her mere presence left him with pounding heart and a drowsy mind with only a fuzzy understanding of sexual emotions.

The women had a separate bathhouse, a tradition that was only afforded by the respected families. Located at the back of their spread out dwelling the small brick floored roofless entity surrounded by bamboo fences was barely a bathhouse. However it did offer some privacy to the women of the family from the gawking public eyes. Maid servants carried water in round clay containers. Even little boys were barred from going there. It was disrespectful and a sin alike. But weren't the rules created to be broken? In an irresistible urge he resigned to his killer curiosity and traveled over the dense hedges with sharp pointed spikes and rotten marshes to make his way to the women's bathhouse. Standing alone, he waited quietly until the right moment came. His heart into his throat, breathing fearfully loud he braved his own cowardice and finally put his eyes on a small hole. Unsuspecting and carefree she hummed a popular song as her beautiful pale hands danced through her clothing, facilitating them to slip through one by one, revealing slowly and steadily the mystery of the universe.

Stunned, he gaped at the amazingly round, smooth and firm entity with a pair of beautifully crafted pink nipples. The unexplainably pretty milky white breasts, so white that they looked almost anemic, momentarily overpowered his body with a unique reaction. His heart still throbbing so hard as to break out of his ribs, he felt an irresistible rising between his legs, unlike any other casual hardening. He sat there frozen, lethargic in the torturous gushing of blood through his body, abnormal but yet so desirable, as the sumptuous feelings resonated through his body, from head to toe, repeatedly.

Then the unthinkable happened. She saw him. This horrifying discovery, to his utter surprise, was met with an indulgent giggle, a touch of embarrassment topped with almost psychiatric patience. She said in a low, jocular voice, "Silly boy! Watching me secretly!"

He leaped away like a cub sensing trouble in a playful hunting session and ran over the hedges, the marshes and into the thick bamboo grove at the backdrop of the village. Still extended and hard, he took his pants off in an attempt to release the uncanny burden, crying silently, anxious about the consequences as his body crept back to normalcy. To his amazement, his fears proved unnecessary. Before boarding her cow pulled cart on her trip back to her home, a days worth of travel, she had hugged him affectionately, whispering secretly into his ears, "Take it easy! It'll be okay!"

Lately, a pretty young woman had won over his affection. Whenever time permitted he arranged meeting with her, often in motels, sometimes in his lonely house. The youngster seemed to like him as well, as she, amid her busy schedule working for an escort service, always found time to be with him. Often she attempted to inundate him with her enviably beautiful, curvy and petite body. She felt obligated to make the generous but melancholy elderly gentleman happy, with only asset she had ever known about - her sensuality. But even her brazen efforts to please him, her tight and luring body, the tanned small but extremely fascinating breasts with all its desired impoliteness, smoothness and sexiness failed to bring back the stormy feelings that once overpowered him in seconds. With soft, expressionless, dreamy eyes he observed the young body, the curves shifted layer to layer, up to bottom, smoothly converting into waves after waves. Like a genius mathematician her body had found an innovative way to mix adorable beauty with her otherwise mundane appearance. When together, his time passed observing her, examining every details of her body, feet to hair, again and again, like a persistent astronomer searching through space for undiscovered celestial bodies. These simple observations illuminated him, something he believed he had never felt even during his happy days with his loving wife. He appreciated the opportunity that life had spared him, once more allowing him to rediscover the beauty and excitement of the world, in his own leisure, in his own terms.

But lately even this young beauty misinterpreted him. He wanted peaceful, quiet company in private settings. No making love, no throbbing hearts, no rummaging through each other's body in unstoppable stimulation. The young woman, confused and lost, had very little clue about his actual needs. Her otherwise risky lifestyle clashed with his demand for candle light dinners with Mozart or Beethoven playing at the background.

Lately, he had been thinking of death. Amusingly, the thought of dying rekindled his desire to live. The hidden resentment and grudge that he fostered over the years had a reverse impact on him. Deep inside, he felt rebellious and silently demanded reconciliation from life, a full phase make out. Nevertheless, he struggled to keep away the bitter memories, to resist the nostalgia, to let the resentment drip out. Despite his tumultuous past he longed his final farewell to come on a tranquil note. But often his fruitless struggles threw him with disdain into even deeper ocean of contempt and sorrow.

Lately, however, just the way at the end of a scorching summer day on a ocean comes the cool, inviting night with its star studded sky and the dark ghostly silhouettes spreading out itself softly with a touch of passion, indulgence and intimacy, the memory of that pair of milky white, extravagantly beautiful and unforgettably exciting breasts emerged silently into his mind. Peeking through a shapeless hole of time he watched the forbidden view with endless fervour. Tears rolled down his eyes as he slowly lost himself in the curious mind of a little silly boy, remembering his first sense of love.

A Family Party

It would be hard to find a family in GTA (Greater Toronto Area) who don't have at least one party during the weekends. Birthdays, marriage anniversaries and religious gatherings are just some of the common events. When none of those are happening then several families may just get together for impromptu parties. After a busy week if the weekend do not present an opportunity to vent out my whole week feels ruined. Okay, I admit, there's another equally important reason for my urge to have such family parties. Our three year old son Zaki happens to be our only child. While he is generally quite entertaining often we – my better half Shili and I – do get exhausted having to play not only the role of his parents but as well as of his friends, uncles, aunts etc. trying hard to eliminate the void in his life as all of our relatives lived far away from us. During the weekdays when school are open the kids keep busy. Parents work, kids study, little time for socializing. The weekend is a different story. The adults seek adult company, the kids of kids.

On this particular evening we were headed for the adobe of our senior friend Jahir and his wife Sufiya. They had vehemently refused to admit that there was any special occasion for the party – a common practice to discourage guests from bringing expensive gifts. However, rarely such camouflages worked as Shili knocked on her secret sources and found out that there was indeed a reason for the party. Our hosts were poised to celebrate their 25th marriage ceremony. Gifts were bought. Generally prudent I wasn't particularly crazy about such acts but I guess every good thing come with a price tag.

When we reached Jahir bhai's home - a townhouse with rows of homes - it was already crowded with dozens of cars taking up every bit of parking spot around the place. Reluctant to steer away too far for a legal parking space I double parked. I planned to inform Jahir bhai just in case the other car needed to get out.

Sufia bhabi cordially received us at the door. Pleasantries exchanged we entered their specious living room only to be surrounded by the gang of the kids who rushed in. This gang consisted of Johny, Shafeen, Raphin, Iti, Bithi and several other kids who I could vaguely recognized. Usually quiet and weary Zaki lightened up instantly. Lately Shili had been working diligently to bolster his social skills. Usually in our circle that meant starting with a measly 'Salam' or 'God Bless you' in Islamic way. However, often making the little ones to do just that turned into an impossible mission. Tonight, just like any other times, the little guy outright refused to utter anything - no matter how much her frustrated mother tried. He wasn't alone. The air filled with the passionate urges from the keen mothers.

"Go ahead dear, say salam to everybody.'
"What's going on? What did I teach you?"
"Say Hi. Please!"
Etc.

The gang instantly froze with total silence following. The childish faces bursting into excitement just moments ago turned blank. Then slowly a few mumbled something ineligibly.

Johny's mom Seema snapped, "Get the hell out of here! When are you hooligans going to learn etiquettes? Can't you even wish a simple salam? Did you guys just lose your voices? Turn up the volume. Say Assalamu Alaikum. No sleepy 'sa..ma..kum."

This brought some half hearted chuckles but no further improvement on the greetings. Once the gang disappeared into the house with their usual vigor Shili shrugged off her disappointment and joined Seema and other ladies. I went on to join the other lads who had gathered there before us. Among several men of middle aged stature I was happy to see some of my close friends. As we met on regular basis we were comfortable together and usually found interesting things to discuss. I noticed some of the families had brought their older kids in the party. Personally since I had turned twelve I thought it was quite embarrassing to accompany my parents anywhere. It was a true pleasure to see these young folks had the heart to come to this party.

Jahir bhai had two sons. Amol older, Atol younger. Both of them had completed their education in commerce and had joined their family business of importing and exporting. Both were amicable, gentle. Time has changed and while just receiving a spontaneous greeting from older kids feels satisfying I actually had a full length conversation with these two. As the party progressed I took special interest in knowing the other young men and women present. I am always fascinated in knowing the upcoming generations.

Monjur bhai and Amina bhabi were both agriculture scientists by education and experience gained back in Bangladesh. Since coming to Canada they had been working as building managers. There wasn't anything wrong with the job particularly but the disagreement between their education and profession could be the cause of heartache for the week hearts. Things aren't supposed to be coming in a platter for new immigrants – it is generally understood. They never complained. They had two children. Daisy – their daughter was studying in journalism in one of the local universities. Riyad – their son was studying in Ottawa, four hours away on car. The parents visited him quite frequently while the young man was kind enough to return the favour at his whim.

Jayed bhai was working as a manager in a departmental store. He was probably a police officer in the past, in our home country. He would not say anything clearly but he surely looked happy and content in a life that evidently did not have anything to do with bribes. His wife Nina however was yet to get used to the life that lacked all the helping hands that she had back home and grudgingly complained at every opportunity. They had two sons – Bashir and Imon. Bashir had been studying to get his PhD in Applied Science while Imon had taken up a temporary job in Indonesia after completing his graduation. He had just returned home after completing his engagement there and was considering multiple full time job offers. Having a degree from a reputable university definitely can make things brighter, especially for the ones who paid any attention in their studies.

However, there are no reasons to believe that

everybody would want the same type of success. Some young men may wonder - what is success anyway? How would one measure success? Why waste time studying for years? Asif - Shihab mama and Bela mami's eldest son - with his ear rings and goatee looked like the horrifying dacoits that we read so much about during our child-hood. There have been too much gang activities around this area in the recent years. I surely hoped Asif haven't signed up with them. His reluctance to education has been a well known fact. He has been working as a cashier in a McDonalds for a little while now. Most of his jobs had been short living. How long McDonalds would interest him that was something we wondered about.

Soon, like every other time, us men got engaged in arguments over Canadian politics. My knowledge in politics had always been very limited but that never stopped me from jumping into discussions. In a nearby dining table Sufia bhabi had arranged all kind of delicious foods. Sensing the presence of saliva dangerously increasing under my tongue I had to quit in my worthless argument. I waited patiently for the call of dinner. The appetizing odour of the food started quite a commotion in my stomach.

That is when I received an invitation to play hide and sick.

Not sure exactly when and how in the past I had the slip of judgement to play hide and seek with the little gang. However, the outcome of such mistake hadn't been very good. Since then in every family gathering this gang seek out for me. I became their perennial seeker while they were obviously the hiders. That was given. The problem was owing to high frequency of family parties which evidently meant plenty of fattening food my midsection had been bulging for a while now and chasing this gang up and down was no more convenient. Yet refusing to play was not a readily available option. Jahir bhai's house was three storied. After several trip up and down I gave up and collapsed in a chair. The gang tried their best to get me back up but I resisted. This was going too far. Finally, frustrated Marufa bitterly said, "Uncle has become old. Look at all the gray hair he has."

That hurt. I only had a few gray hairs in my sideburns. That surely couldn't be considered as a sign of oldness.

Once the kids disappeared I furtively looked at the dining table. It was overwhelmed with all kind of eye popping, mouth watering delicious foods. How long does a man have to wait for a meal? My patience was about to break. I felt like singing out the famous song of Tagor, "Open the door o' dear; why make me wait so long?"

Who knew the door was about to get totally nailed.

I heard a big commotion generating from the family room where the ladies had gathered. Rushing in I was appalled to find out our hostess Sufia bhabi have passed out. She had diabetes and possibly high blood pressure. All the cooking she had done earlier the day to feed her guests must had been very stressful on her. After plenty of water splashed on her face when she did not come back emergency services was called. The ambulance showed up in no time. Not sure if it was the red-blue lights of the ambulance or the cold air but right before she was to be loaded into the ambulance Sufia bhabi became awake, immediately jumped out from her stretcher and looked around with total surprise.

"What's wrong? What are you all looking at?"

It couldn't have been more than five minutes after the departure of the ambulance when she passed out for the second time. However water did its magic this time. She was awake but unable to get out of her bed. In all these chaos the food had turned ice cold. I doubted if I was the only one among all guests who felt the churning in the stomach known as 'hunger' but nobody surely wasn't saying anything, not at a time like this. Not knowing when we'll be out of this troubling situation I allowed myself to grab couple of chicken roasts stealthily at the first opportunity that came. I then secretly slipped out to the backyard and obliterated them in record time.

Delayed but not omitted dinner was eventually served. Sufia bhabi forced her out of the bed and looked after the proceeding with shaky legs and apologizing words. Jahir bhai flanked to her in this quest just in case things get uncomfortable again.

The party broke late, around half past one in the morning, like all our family parties. Surprisingly we found all the kids, regardless of their age and size, fully awake and in high spirit. Under normal circumstances this was way beyond their bed times. However, once in the car and strapped securely on their seats they usually dozed off. Today was no exception. Zaki was asleep before we barely passed the nearest curb.

As we drove back a healthy late night traffic kept us company.

This city never sleeps.

The Wall

I waited well into the dinner before dropping the news.

"I think I am ready for marriage."

I, Shafi Ahmed, a Nuclear Physicist, worked as a researching scientist for a reputed company. At 30 I was still single and lived with my parents, as I had all my life.

It was a regular family dinner, the only meal in the day when we sat around our oversized dinner table and ate together. Emigrated from Dhaka several decades ago, my parents diligently practiced some traditions over the years that they deemed as part of our Bangladeshi culture. One of them was, obviously, having dinner together. Not my favorite time, but obedience was supposedly another sought out tradition.

My dad, a reputed businessman, was picking out the tiny bones of a piece of hilsa - a popular fish back home that we bought frozen from local Bangladeshi groceries, his both hands occupied in the task, threw me a quick glance before concentrating back on the bones.

"Finally! Your mother has been waiting for this moment so long. She'll find a beautiful bride for you."

Now, that was part of tradition as well. In my community, not strictly but preferably, children were expected to allow their parents to arrange their marriages.

It wasn't as bad as it sounded, considering the long living marriages, mostly happy, that most of our parents had.

My mother - kind hearted, soft-spoken, couldn't-be-more-naïve - looked at me with exploding eyes. "Really? I thought you didn't like marriage."

"I changed my mind."

The college going twin sisters – Poly and Dolly – exclaimed in unison," You are the best, bhaiya! Finally doing the right thing! We'll have a sister-in-law in the house! It's going to be so much fun!"

Dad defeated the mighty fish bones. His eyes glistened in success.

"You are not going to change your mind again, are you?"

"No, no. I am determined this time."

"Great! Your mother was losing sleep over this. Now dear, go crazy."

"Don't be silly." Mom shyly said. "I already have my eyes set on somebody."

"Not Choudhury's ugly daughter?" Dad asked.

"Are you nuts? Who would want her? I was talking about Selim Sahib's daughter."

"Rita apu?" Poly-Dolly asked.

"Yes! What a wonderful girl! Pretty, nice, smart, educated." Mom dreamily said.

"I like somebody." I muttered.

Mom turned anemic. "Oh! Who is she? You never told us anything about her."

"I met her just recently"

"Oh! Who is she?" Mom was impatient.

"Her name is Jessica Ganga."

"Race?" Dad asked, laboring hard not to show his emotions.

"Does it matter?" I let the words slip through my lips.

"May be not. I still want to know."

"Canadian."

"Don't get smart on me." Dad raised his voice considerably.

"Caribbean. "

"Black?" Mom sweated.

"Is that a problem, mom?" I tried not to sound rude. The last time I raised my voice at her she cried for two days, didn't talk to me for one whole week.

"I didn't say that. But you know how people appreciates light skin in our community." Mom spoke her heart. She looked worried.

"I guess a Caucasian would work for you." I said, perhaps a little too rudely than I wanted.

"I was thinking Rita. You should see her. She is so light skinned!" Mom was dreamy again.

"You should look at your own daughters." I had to point out. "They are not exactly milky."

None of us were, except mom.

"Shame on you, bhaiya! How can you speak like that about us?"

They can be very aggressive when they wanted. I surrendered.

Dad didn't like Rita, I knew. He showed some interest in Jessica.

"What does her father do? Where do they live?"

"Her father passed away last year. I never asked about his profession. Jessica lives in Ajax."

"She works?"

"Part time."

"Who handle the finances?"

"She does. Her mother has Alzheimer. She can't work."

"Any siblings?"

"A brother who is in the army. He is married with kids."

"What kind of work is she doing?"

I cleared my voice. "Waitress. In a bar."

Dad furrowed his eyebrows deeply before jumping out of his chair with disbelief. "What!"

"Are you out of your mind?" Mom was equally embarrassed.

"Gosh! " My sisters gasped.

"Why are you guys acting like that? She is not a showgirl or anything." It was not unexpected but I had to act.

"What's the difference?" Dad displayed four familiar wrinkles on his forehead. "At least that pays way better."

Mom was the first one to calm down. "How does she look?"

"Don't think Bollywood, Hollywood."

"Complexion? " Mom hesitantly asked, fearing my wrath.

"Brown. Light brown. Kind of like us."

"What is she studying?" That was dad.

"Office administration, in a community college."

"Why couldn't she find a better job?" Mom was genuinely concerned.

"What's wrong with her current job? She makes

good money."

Mom remained silent as she played with her food.

Dad sat down, took a deep breath. "Forget about her. I'll speak to Rita's dad tomorrow. It will be a good match."

"I plan to marry Jessica." I braved.

Poly-Dolly usually favored me.   Not this time. "Come on, bhaiya. She is not that bright!"

I ignored them. They could be nerve wrecking annoying sometimes.

Dad gave me one of his famous fiery looks. "Any comments on that?"

"Her circumstances were not exactly favorable. She is a smart girl." I tried to keep it in perspective.

"Don't you want to consider our position in the society?"

"I don't see anything to be embarrassed of."

"You don't? We'll become a common joke among our peers. They would laugh at our back. Just last month my business partner Akmal got his son married to a lady doctor. If nothing else you could at least consider higher education."

"Perhaps you need to reevaluate the company you keep. Friends don't laugh at your back."

"Don't you lecture me! You know what I mean. We'll have little choice but to avoid gatherings. Don't you realize how humiliating it will be?" There was an urge in my dad's tone, almost like pleading. This wasn't something I was used to see of him. I sort of enjoyed it.

"We don't plan to stay in this house. Nobody

would even see us. You'll be fine."

Dad gave me a scorching look before stomping into his bedroom. I knew he was going to call mom's big brother, Kasem, his mentor and friend.

"Kashem? Can you stop by A.S.A.P? Very urgent. Your nephew is planning to ruin us. He is talking about marrying a waitress form a bar! Either you stop him or bring a strong nylon rope for me. I'll end this life…."

"This is not good." Mom coldly said.

Poly-Dolly rolled their eyes in disgust.

Uncle Kashem had a reputation for being very prompt. He lived at the east end of Scarborough but managed to show up in Richmond Hill, where we lived, a forty plus kilometer distance, in less than thirty minutes.

He came in with his trademark big smile. "Don't worry. I'll set everything right."

I knew things were going to get down slope from here. He was notorious for that. To make things even worse he brought his wife Shahina and my father's younger sister Bina and her husband Jafor, who lived near him. Standing before the curious audience dad went berserk. He threw his arms in the air, turned his volume high and issued a fiery speech – he would rather cut his only son into pieces and feed the pieces to the about-to-be extinct Royal Bengal Tiger then to allow this unacceptable marriage.

Uncle Kashem broke into laughter. "Brother, you haven't changed a bit. Don't you get a simple joke? Do you think our Shafi would do something so stupid? Don't you know your own son? He is like the smartest kid in the family. He knows what is good for him. He was just pulling your leg. Ha…ha…ha…"

Uncle Jafor, a full professor in a reputed university, was not a total loss. "What's so wrong with this girl?" He thoughtfully said. "She is studying, working. Sounds good."

Dad snapped. "You have a son old enough for marriage. Why don't you take her?"

"Well, I see no harm in it. If my son agrees we can pursue."

I had to step in. Didn't like the way it was heading. "There's no need for that uncle Jafor. I am getting married to her."

Aunt Bina was a true copy of dad, only belonged in the opposite gender. She and dad shared same temperament as well. "Don't be a foolhardy." She barked.

"I love her. I told her I want to marry her. I can't back off now." I tried to explain my situation to avoid the onslaught.

Uncle Kashem broke into another laughter. "So what? I did the same with several girls before getting married to your aunt. What's the big deal?"

His wife, Shahina, chuckled. "Don't you lie. You were shy like a teenage girl."

They knew each other and had a mild affair of the hearts. We have heard that story too many times.

Poly-Dolly loved anything that smelled like love. They giggled. "Come on aunt Shahina, tell us more."

"Be quiet." Dad yelled at the twins. "We didn't gather here to listen to some prehistoric love affair. Let's talk about my son."

Uncle Kashem relaxed into his chair. "Give me few days. I'll find you the prettiest angel. We'll get this kid married by next Friday."

Mom interrupted. "There's no need to look. I already have one. Selim Sahib's daughter - Rita. We like her very much."

Aunt Shahina frowned. "Really? How much do you know about her? I heard she had several boyfriends over the years."

"What?" Mom must have missed a series of heart beats. "Who told you that?"

"Does it matter? I myself saw her with a boy once. They were – you know – intimate, in a mall. Kissing-issing!"

"Oh god!" Mom shrieked. "And I was visualizing her as the deity of my household. What is happening to our kids? We never dared to do anything like this when we were young."

"Forget about Rita." Uncle Kashem declared. "Allow me to find you a daughter-in-law. She will be everything that you dreamed of. Top class."

Mom sighed deeply. "Do what you think best, bhaiya."

I noticed aunt Shahina smiling at me. She was the type who said less and did more. When in trouble she could be a big help. I recollected some of my courage. "You guys should at least check Jessica out."

"Forget Jessica. She has no social status. Your family has a respectable position in the community. Don't forget that. There's nothing to see here." Dad was quick to dismiss.

"Don't be so narrow minded dad." I objected.

Aunt Bina was quick to lose her temper as well. "I am yet to meet another rascal like you." She snarled. "She is nobody. Why are you so determined to marry her? Are you out of your mind?"

"Who cares what he wants?" Dad declared boldly. "Kashem, we'll have to get him married tomorrow."

"Tomorrow? What about the bride? Where am I going to find a bride at this hour? Do you expect me to go door to door and look for a suitable bride? Ha...ha...ha..."

"Stop! Don't laugh like a bed bug." Dad snapped.

"Brother, you are turning into a genius. You even figured out how the bed bugs laugh! Do they really laugh?"

Aunt Bina had a different idea going on in her fertile mind. "My daughter Daisy likes him a lot." She said. "She is pretty and smart. Why don't we get the two of them tie the knots?"

I grimaced. We grew up together like siblings. What was wrong with this lady?

Uncle Kasem readily objected. "What do you take us for? Your daughter is no better than Rita. Since high school she must have changed three boyfriends. There's barely anybody who doesn't know about her romantic extravaganzas."

"Come on Kasem bhaiya, boyfriends are not husbands. Who cares if she had three or thirty?" Aunt Bina reasoned.

"Why not Rita then?"

Nobody replied. Mom said, "What other choices we have?"

Uncle Kasem cleared his voice. "Well, why aren't you considering my daughter Shila. Go find a girl like her. A living goddess."

There was a momentary silence in the room.

"But when I proposed you last time you got really mad at me." Mom was truly surprised.

"Forget about what I did last time. When almighty wants something who are we to object? Let's get it settled right now."

Gosh! Were these people nuts! Shila discussed her love interests with me. That's the type of closeness we had.

Aunt Bina strongly objected. "How is Daisy any less than her? Shila isn't half as pretty as my Daisy."

Uncle Kasem went all ballistic. "What are you talking about? Do you know how many guys goofs around just to see Shila smile?"

"Smile, my foot." Aunt Bina chewed out the words. "Such shovel teeth!"

Mom liked Shila. She objected. "Don't be silly Bina. She has perfectly good teeth."

Uncle Jafor agreed. "True. Such a nice girl. Whenever I go she makes me her especial barbeque chicken."

"Shut up!" Aunt Bina barked at him. "We are talking about two lives and he is reminiscing barbeque chicken! Listen bhaiya, Shafi and Daisy would make a great couple. There's no need to get out of our own family. "

This got mom going. She furiously said, "Why, what's wrong with our family? Do you know my grandfather's grandfather was a king?"

Poly-Dolly readily supported. "Yes aunt Bina, his name was King Shofed Ali Shorder. We even saw his picture. So cute! Oh my god!"

"We also have dozens of such good-for-nothing

kings in our family tree." Aunt Bina slapped in the air, disdainfully. "We are not here to discuss that. Shafi is getting married with Daisy. That's final."

Mom was trembling in anger. She shouted, "Never. Shafi will get married with Shila."

"Let bhaiya decide."

"Oh well!" dad scrambled for appropriate words.

"What do you want me to say?"

Aunt Shahina softly said, "Let's all calm down for a minute. Marriage is not a game."

"Of course not." Dad scratched his head. He feared his little sister. "What do you say Kashem? Who is better? Shila or Daisy?"

"Daisy doesn't even come close."

"How dare you?" Aunt Bina lashed out. "Whole Shila doesn't stand a chance against a single toe of Daisy."

"Watch it Bina!" Uncle Kashem wasn't stepping back.

"Don't you threat me. You think we don't know what you are up to? Your eyes are on my brother's property, especially now that his real estate business have picked up. Can you deny that?"

Uncle Kasem jumped up from his seat. "How dare you say that? Do I have any less?"

Uncle Jafor begged, "Please stop. This is going too far."

Aunt Bina threw her arms in the air. "Don't you worry. I know how to deal with thugs like him."

Dad nervously said, "There's no need to fight over this."

None of the two warring parties paid any attention to him.

I had no clue where this was heading to. I stood there helplessly. It was remarkable to notice how a simple situation could turn into a feud. Aunt Shaina was looking at me. As I met her eyes she signaled me out of the room. I quietly slipped out to the porch. Moments later she joined me there. She was all smiles.

"Son, when did you get married?"

"Three days ago."

"Where is Jessica?"

"In her house."

"I don't think you can bring her here. Not now." She thoughtfully said.

"I just wanted their blessings."

"Well, that's not going to happen too soon. You realize that."

"What should I do?"

"What else? Just go on with your life. You have a good job. You two will do great by yourself."

"She is such a terrific girl! She would win you in seconds."

"I know that. If she was any less you wouldn't go for her. Now, get out of here. Once they stop fighting they are going to look for you. Spend a few days away. When things calm down come back to get your stuff. I'll manage these old kids. It will be okay."

"What about mom and dad?"

"Worry about them later. Parents loves to have opportunities to forgive their children. You just have to come and beg for it. Now go on. I'll handle them for now."

I touched her toes three times, an age-old Indian tradition to show respect. "Pray for us Aunt."

"You can count on that. Go now. Quick."

I left home empty handed. The mansion, the wealth, the expensive lifestyle that I got so used to, all stayed behind. But yet I felt so good. I thought of Jessica, drew picture of a happy home, a healthy cute baby in our lives – my heart flooded with immense pleasure. As I walked to the curb where my car was parked I turned back to get a glimpse of Aunt Shahina, who still stood on the porch, smiling. Behind her now stood my mom, grim faced, concerned, loose end of her sari waved like a flag in a sudden gust of wind, as if to say, "Go on son. Break the walls."

The Intriguing Melody
(Tale of the Old land)

There was barely any warning before the dark fluid monster rushed through the pitch-black night flashing its killer claws. The village, located in a flood prone corner of Bangladesh, was suddenly pulled into life from the uncanny quietness that shrouded it.

Sitting on his porch folklore singer Nijam was trying out different tunes on his two-string, keeping it low. He was the one to notice it first. A singer and philosopher, nothing in life stroke him as very important or serious. He called out for his wife in a rather trifling voice, "Simul's mom, there comes the water. The dam must have given away."

Nuri couldn't sleep. She had miserable headache since evening. She was lying on the bed messaging her throbbing head. Hearing the warning, she instantly jumped out of the bed and screamed at the top of her voice, "Flood! Flood! Get up Shimul. The water is here."
One scream proved enough. The village woke up in a blink of eye. Everybody knew the flood was coming. The only hope was the dam. It wasn't anything fancy. An old, shaky structure but still it was there. They feared often that the ferocious current would blow the poor thing

away in one moment's forceful push and rush toward the village with all its might. Tonight was the night. The dam broke; the deadly sharks swam with their wavy, smooth bodies, flashing their sharp bloodthirsty liquid teeth.

The first burst of sweeping water flooded Nijam's yard. Hypnotic, Nijam observed – O' Mother Nature! Look at the power, the strength and the unimaginable beauty you hold! Cold water touched him, his cloths get soaked, and yet he couldn't move. He just sat there with his mind spilling with heart wrenching fillings.

Nuri was a smart woman. She quickly realized the graveness of the situation. Forcing Shimul out of bed, she packed up some rice and lintel in a jute bag and some cloths in another. Handing over the cloths to Shimul she fetched out the money that she was saving in a small cavity inside a bamboo stick.

The whole village was drowned in chaos, as if the fearsome dacoits had hit. The water level was rising fast, the current becoming forceful, the yards of the mud houses going under, the clusters of paddy drowning. The numerous, untimely call for prayers, a traditional response to disasters, echoed the air; the neighbor's infant baby cried with her lungs out; people cautioned each other. All these noises were easily buried by the ominous howling of the flooding water.

Holding her daughter's hand, Nuri stepped out on the yard. She stared at her husband softly. "Let's go Simul's dad. We need to move out before it's too late. Water is going to rise. Everything will float away. Come on, let's go. "

Nijam had unconditional love for his wife. He often wondered how this beautiful, quiet woman managed the innumerable issues with the daily life so calmly, never bothering him with anything. He followed his wife and daughter quietly.

Dozens of families had gathered together in knee-deep water. The village school located south on a hill was less likely to get underwater. That was their destination. Before they started, they checked for the last time to ensure all the family members were with them. The men shouted, children cried, elderly screamed, poultry cackled and cattle lowed. Once a head count confirmed everybody's presence, a few young men with lanterns in their hands leaded the group ahead. They all talked, about the flood, about the houses they left behind, about the unripe clusters of the paddy; the elderly even got into an argument over the correct time line about another big flood in the past. Nijam, following the group, oblivious to his surroundings, unmindfully played his fingers over the wires of his two-string, ding...ding...ding...!

The schoolhouse was a small mud structure with hay roof. Everyday a few kids gathered here with their slates and chalks while an otherwise useless man with an S.S.C. certification taught them how to read Bengali alphabets in a high, rhythmic chorus. There was a promise for the school to be extended, more rooms, blackboards, and free supplies for the kids. It proved to be another hollow promise of Chairman Hedayet Ali, who never ran out of excuses to divert people's attention from it.

This unfortunate, barely standing structure called the schoolhouse became the final shelter for the group, a few families with too many members. The clouds packed

115

the sky; wind pushed harder; current became stronger. The river spilled out with even further vigor, the earth sunk, the poor villagers were reduced to bare minimum existence.

Nijam maintained a distance from the crowd. Shimul flanked him, quiet as ever. Like her father she spoke less, preferred solitude. Staying nearby, Nuri conversed whisperingly to Ali's wife Jinnat, keeping an eye on her husband and daughter.

The families sat scattered inside the schoolhouse, a fog of melancholy bore its imprint on their faces. The initial excitement was gone; the thought of future shrouded their minds. The children, restless and hungry, cried sporadically as the helpless mothers scolded them to quietness; the able bodied small but muscular fathers stared at the deep dark circulating water with expressionless eyes as they puffed frequently on their handmade cigarettes and breathed out the cloud of poisonous smoke.

Umor Mia had enough with such strenuous silence. He threw the cigarette stub in the water, watched it driven away quickly. The rising water level couldn't hide the inevitable from his sharp eyes. The devil was stepping up to them, slowly but surely. He yelled like a lonely midnight fox, "Guys, what's the use of sitting like dead? Can't you see the water level rising? Do you want to get buried here with your families? "

He glared at everyone. Some of the men moved uneasily, their faces hardly visible in the weak light of the lanterns, expressions still hidden. The children watched keenly giving the pointless crying a break. Umor enjoyed the attention. He yelled with even more enthusiasm, "Get up guys! Let's get out of here before the water reaches us."

He however restrained from giving any specific solution. The water level was now at least up to the chest of a grown man. It was next to impossible to take the kids and the elderly to safety through such deep water.

The silence prevailed. Ignored and irked Umor burst out, "What's the matter? Why don't you say anything?"

Umor had a reputation as a thief. He had never been caught but sudden presence of wealth in his otherwise poverty ridden dwelling gave people ideas.

Taleb, Roushan, Samad, and Abed – none of them liked Umor much. They themselves weren't any saints. In fact they frequently stole bags of rice from their employer's storage whenever the opportunity knocked. But yet, they were not considered thieves.

"Shut up, bloody thief," yelled back Taleb. "Let the water rise. Who hasn't sinned has nothing to worry about."

Umor objected vigorously, "Don't dare call me a thief. Did you ever see me stealing?"

Taleb shouted back, "Who in the village doesn't know that you are a thief? What's there to see here? When we have hard time feeding our families, you are having three hot meals! Where do you get so much supply?"

"That's not your headache. I take from the stinking rich, the ones that suck our blood to build their empires. There's nothing wrong in robbing them." On the spur of moment Umor did not realize what he was saying.

Samad chuckled. "There you go - a full confession finally. You son of a thief, keep your big mouth sealed."

"Watch your mouth, Samad. Don't you dare swear at me!"

"Oh, no? What are you going to do...huh...?"

He couldn't finish his words before Umor threw his body on him in a mad dash. Grabbing each other by the torso they rolled on the dirt floor, growling in rage, as the rest hesitantly watched the two men take it on each other, a few half heartedly attempting to separate them. The dozing children startled back into their crying feat, the women screamed, the elderly offered their trembling advice; Nijam Baul touched his strings – ding...dong, as the rushing river continued in its aggression.

Nijam really wanted to put his mind into completing the unfinished tune, but he could barely concentrate. His mind was restless. The endless gatherings of the dark, cottony clouds had surprisingly allowed a few stars to glitter through, the random striking of the lightning brought in the fearsome thunders, the darkness to the brightness, the silence to the deafening noise, all these collectively blew his mind away – he saw, he heard, his mind filled with the beauty and glamour of this mother earth, of that infinite sky! There was music in the water; there was music in the clouds; there was music in the stars! Oh, the kind one, the great one, what a wonder have you created! It was the right moment to observe, to feel, not to waste time on trivial music.

The water kept on rising, as if it had desired to

gulp the schoolhouse. The adults continued to watch its progress with blunt emotion. A few adventurous kids braved playing hide and seek. They were put to their senses mercilessly. Scolded and beaten the kids joined in a chorus of cry, their collective noise attempted to challenge the roaring of the clouds in vein.

Sobhan, a strong, descent looking farmer hand, had a feelings going for Lili, daughter of one Naimuddin, for a while. He hadn't uttered the word of love yet but frequently thought about it. Lily, a pretty and lively girl at fourteen, was just as much in love with Sobhan. Noticing him standing alone Lily slowly walked to Sobhan. "Hi!"
Clearly pleased in her presence, Sobhan shyly said, "Are you okay, Lili?"

"The water level keeps on rising. We can't stay here too long", Lili said almost as a casual observation. There was no real anxiousness in her voice. All she cared now was to be near Sobhan.

Sobhan hold her hand softly. Lili quickly looked around. Finding nobody noticing them she dared another step closure to him.

"Don't be scared. We'll find a way out." Sobhan sounded low, passionate. His fingers played hers; a fresh and joyous energy soothingly flew between them.

"I am not scared. I fear nothing when I am with you."

A strange feeling of happiness made Sobhan almost lethargic. He even had the luxury to dream of a sweet future with her. "Lili, next year, I am going to ask your hand in marriage, I promise."

Sobhan knew it was a hopeless dream. He had to

support his sick mother, two teenage sisters and old granny. Poverty had no patience for dreams.

Lili, moving even further intimately whispered, "Someday we'll be together."

Suddenly Naimuddin, Lili's father, darted toward them. Pushing Lili away from Sobhan he barked, "I see you trying to seduce her one more time I'll cut you."

Hurt by such unholy interpretation Sobhan said, "Uncle Naimuddin, I love Lili. I plan to ask her hand in marriage."

Noimiddin came dashing like a bull, intending to tear the youth off with his horn less head. Sobhan stood his ground, braced Naimuddin with his strong arms as he wrestled to get free, finally pushing him into the water. Naimuddin, calmed down, struggled up from the water and walked away in disgrace. Sobhan tried to read Lili's reaction. In the dark he could hardly see her face, let alone the emotions.

The water marched up, about to touch the floor. The silent figures moved back anxiously, danger was imminent. Such danger hadn't come for so long now. One elderly woman cried out, "Take the name of Almighty you all; take the name of the Allah." Someone called out for prayer at the top his voice.

Jinnat, a woman in her early twenties, wept silently. Timid and softhearted she only confided in Nuri, who guided her like a big sister. Caressing Jinnat's hair, Nuri said, "Be strong, dear."

Jinnat sobbed hopelessly. "Sister Nuri, I can't take it anymore. He hits me all the time, no matter what I do. If I talk I get smacked, if I don't I get smacked. There's no love, no respect. How long can I cop up with this? "

"But Ali was never like this. I know him for so long now."

"How would you know anybody looking from a distant? Inside he is a pure devil, a greedy monster. He keeps asking my dad for more dowries, beats me brutally when refused. My father has no means to comply. All my ornaments are already sold. There's nothing more I can give him. What am I going to do?"

The plethora of sorrow that had been gathering dust deep inside Jinnat seemed to find a way out, her hopeless and apparently futureless life with all its relentless agony made her insensitive to the approaching danger. Just one year after marriage, her life turned into a complete void, a pure worthless existence.

"I want to die, sister, I just want to die." Jinnat burst into tears.

Nuri, tears in her eyes, pulled Jinnat close, lovingly. "Don't say such stupid things, dear. Allah will be offended. Only he has the power to take us back."

"What's the use of living like this, sister?"
Nuri didn't have an answer for her. She just sat there silently, embracing her. One could hear Nijam Baul's two-string rang uncertainly ...ding...dong...

The clouds thundered, lightning pierced, water rose, further and further, covered the floor of the schoolhouse. The women wailed, men became restless, the children silent in anticipation, the elderly cried out the name of the creator. One little girl, seeing her mother weeping tried to wipe out the tears, "Don't cry mother. Why do you cry?"

And then, right at that moment, Nijam Baul found the tune he was searching for. He felt as if in the command of a super power the discord that persisted among the sky, the wind and the water had merged into a single harmony taking the shape of something unimaginably big. He observed the dancing waves; he observed the floating clouds; he observed the distant, quiet darkness; his whole heart filled with the music of infinity; the beauty of the creator reflected through the shadowy creations. His fingers moved spontaneously on the two-string, the simple ding...dong... started to take the form of an actual tune. Keeping his voice in tuned with the wild nature around he first started to hum, soon, inadvertently Nijam's voice rose, it rose until it surpassed the howling of the current, wailing of the wind and roaring of the lightning – the song of little, insignificant men offering his love for the immortal One.

Total Loser

It was a beautiful sunny summer day and there was no reason for any of us to believe that it could somehow turn into a pleasing nightmare. If you are having difficulty grasping the idea of a nightmare being pleasing just wait until I have taken you through it.

There is little doubt over the fact that summer in Toronto is awfully short. There is so much to do but so little time. One of our favorite activities has been to visit beaches, usually in large groups. We are firm believers of plurality. Anyway, on this particular day we - six families - headed for Darlington Provincial Park conveniently located near the Town of Courtice, not too far from Toronto. This was our first visit to this park despite the fact that it was literally next to our home in Ajax – a Toronto suburb, less than twenty minutes away. Once again Tagore, the Nobel winning Indian laureate, proved himself right as he had skillfully wrote in his poem: We have seen so much but not the drop of mist that collects on a blade of grass just off the porch.

It was already past noon when we finally made it to the park. Getting the kids ready, packing up the essentials including but not limited to food, cloths etc. and the morning becomes a matter of past. But the summer days here are satisfyingly long with light hovering around as late as 9 in the evening. A little late start wasn't going to ruin anything. We had plenty of time.

Darlington Park is located by the shore of Lake Ontario. It has a nice sandy shallow beach, perfect for kids to go crazy. Just west of the beach is McLaughlin bay, a water body that is heavily forested in most sides and separated from the larger waves of Lake Ontario by a narrow patch of sandy zone with a small opening. This is why there is barely any current in McLaughlin bay most part of the day. In the area where the bay meets the beach water is so calm that it has become a popular spot for a leisurely rowing experience. The park authority has built a boat rental stall near that location – something that I had noticed as soon as I arrived there. They had mostly wooden canoes with a few foot paddle boats.

Proud owner of an inflatable boat and a pump I carried both with me wherever I went in summer. Inflating the boat usually took less than five minutes. No question it was not meant to compete with the fancy looking canoes but it floated just fine and carried three people without any problem. Instead of wasting money on canoe rental I used it wherever situation permitted. Such saving may seem insignificant but over time the savings did look good. Anyway, considering the fact that we paid such a large portion of our income in taxes any kind of savings worked.

Along with the boat I carried a tent with me as well. Thanks to modern technology - a complete tent setup can be carried in a small bag. Parachute cloth with fiberglass poles – a tent can be set up in just minutes. A very useful thing to carry if there are little kids in the party. They almost evidently need to take an afternoon nap. The tent worked as a nice, safe shelter. Sometimes ladies joined them as well to avoid the scorching sun. Most of our wives, if not all, are devoted Muslims and go to the beach with most part of their bodies covered. Among all the scantily dressed women enjoying the bright sun in a beach they look like Christian nuns. Sometimes if they feel like they may walk along the beach occasionally stepping into the water to get their feet wet. No amount of deriding can make them steer away from this routine. Often when everybody else is out there in the water or on the beach enjoying the beautiful sunshine these ladies escape in the privacy of the tent and rest or nap. My better half is no exception.

Liton mama, who is my university friend Ferdaus's maternal uncle (mamu is the term for maternal uncles), and his brother in law Elis had joined us in this day out. Both are in their early forties and have children of tender age. As soon as I set the tent up they anchored near it. Displaying enough sign of intelligence I almost always - situation permitting - set the tent near the sand so that the kids can play while being in the line of sight of the parents who don't want to have anything to do with sand, sun or water and can rest near the tent.

Ferdaus and Hasan - two of my close friends from university lived in the big city and had joined me with their families in this expedition, pun intended. All together plenty of kids, all of them looked excited, happy and eager to get on with the beach routines. We quickly snacked on the food that we carried in and while kids and men ran to the beach women took shelter under a tree near the tent. The sun was blazing, water was warm, a breeze blew - it was very soothing for both the body and the mind. After spending a good hour in the beach – swimming, digging and numerous water wars with the kids - when we returned to the tent our appetite were sky high. Our ladies, each excellent cook, had brought cooked delicious food from home, which they gracefully served. Each participating family brought predetermined food items to be shared with others – a tradition that we follow diligently to keep the overall experience interesting and appetizing. I am a sucker for potlucks as it always deliver much more varieties and flavors. My mouth watered up just smelling the delicious foods. A devoted consumer of food I have been trying hard to rein in on my eating habits lately as I race past 40 and noticed the uprise of my midsection. However, rich, delicious food and counting calories do not go together. I try to keep such unwelcome thoughts far back of my mind during these outings.

After the meal, better described as a feast, we spent some time discussing our next plans – go back on the beach or go for boating. Lightly baked under the scorching sun I was secretly fostering the hope to be able to get an afternoon nap inside the tent and recoup but the kids weren't about to let something like that to happen. They were dying to be on the inflatable boat.

Once inflated I put the boat on the capable shoulders of the kids and led them to the McLaughlin bay pushing through the unusually heavy foot crowd. Hasan along with his two daughters followed us as well. His older daughter Tapoti was fourteen, the younger one Obilia – the little dancing star of Toronto's Bangladeshi community was 4. Both of them seemed eager to hop into the boat. My two kids – Zaki and Far had been at the forefront. Ferdaus's daughter Ivana who was eleven held up the center of the boat. Far behind came in a turtle pace the wives of Ferdaus, Hasan and mine – namely Munni, Jerin and Shili. Liton mama and Elis had shown their interest in joining us at the bay but not before their young ones had a chance to take a short nap so that they could rejuvenate. Ferdaus was walking along the beach chasing his one year old son who had some kind of extraordinary fascination for water bodies. Once the boy had enough he would join us as well.

McLaughlin bay looked like a huge pond. At one end it was narrow but as it moved eastward it eventually widened up to a distance of quarter of a mile end to end. The boat ramp was next to the boat rental place. It was packed with boats trying to get into the bay. We tried in vain to find a spot to float our boat. Realizing things wasn't about to get any better as more people flocked in the boat rental place we moved further down the shoreline and found ourselves a shallow and isolated spot. The current was very mild in that part allowing various types of Water lilies and several other water plants to grow in abundance. Many of them had bloomed profusely.

The chaos and confusion that followed once I had floated the boat might surprise or even shock some but I had seen enough of that. The kids started a noisy bickering trying to settle the riding order. I knew something like this would happen, it almost always did. The boat could take three adults or four-five kids if they could fit in. However I carry only one adult life jacket and two for kids. That limitation worked well to manage the load. I was the boatman leaving room for two kids. As the bickering continued I waited patiently hoping for them to settle it themselves. After several more minutes of screaming, yelling and crying they finally calmed down. After some more discussions they all agreed that Ivana and Far would go first, Zaki and Tapoti next and then Obilia with her dad.

The first two trips went quite well. I have two oars. They can be inserted inside two rings attached to the boat for better stroke. In calm water it is quite easy to control the boat however with current it can become very challenging. I have been doing it for a while and have sufficient expertise to handle rough situations. I took the kids around for a little bit, got them close enough to the water lilies so that they could pick one or two up and then dropped them to the shore. Tapoti had been very eager to row so I allowed her to try it out for a little bit. Initially the boat went in a circle several times but then she seemed to get the hang of it and the boat stabilized. It was good to see her enthusiasm. Rowing is harder than it looks. However, what followed next was not something I was prepared for.

Hasan and Obilia's turn was next. The problem arose with Hasan. He was a good swimmer but I still did not want him to ride without a life jacket. I could give him mine but he had never done any rowing and did not look comfortable with the idea of managing the boat all by himself. However, equipped with the brief practice that she got just minutes ago Tapoti looked quite confident and offered to take over the boat from me. Assuming there weren't much that could happen in such calm water I allowed this young lady to captain the inflatable. Obilia knew nothing about swimming but she had little fear of anything, let alone water. She was the first one to jump in the boat and settle in one side. Hasan struggled into my life jacket and very carefully climbed into the boat. With her passengers boarded Tapoti, now the captain of the boat, pushed ahead with a stroke of her paddle. The boat slid through the calm blue water of McLaughlin bay effortlessly. Happy to see that the father and the daughters were out to have a really good time I picked up my fishing rod and walked a short distance away along the shoreline in search of a good spot to try out my luck.

After walking a few hundred yards I found a little opening in the densely grown bushes and small trees giving me just enough room to cast. I tried for a while with no luck, not even a single bite. I moved even further down the shore, away from the boat ramp. I could not see Hasan and his daughters on the boat from where I stood and assumed that they must have had returned to the land by then.

Suddenly I heard Shili calling out for me. Call of urgency. I ran out of the bushes. She looked worried. What she told me that didn't sound like something to be awfully concerned about. Yet just to see it in my own eyes I accompanied her back to the boat ramp. What I saw was exactly what Shili had described. The inflatable was floating about couple of hundred yards from the shore with Hasan and his two daughters on it and seemed to be slowly drifting away.

" How did they manage to go that far?" I asked rather curiously. "I thought I asked them to stay near the shore."

Jerin bhabi who was watching the development

very anxiously responded, "They didn't want to go. The boat just floated that way."

"The wind has been strong." Shili added. "They are trying to come back to the shore for a while now but to no avail. Why don't you rent a boat and help them back?"

The boat rental would close at six. It was ten minutes to six.

Shili rushed me. "What are you waiting for?"

I was not very keen on wasting a whole bunch of money on the rental, unnecessarily. Okay, they were a little away from the shore but wasn't really in any kind of immediate danger. Little Obilia was even smiling and waving cheerfully. Obviously she was not sharing the anxiousness of her father and older sister to return on land. Two of them had been rowing diligently at least for twenty minutes and both were tired by now. Father and daughter might even had a little argument over the odd situation as I could hear Tapoti breaking into short burst of rants at random interval. The distance was considerable and they spoke in a dialect used in Sylhet – a province of Bangladesh, but still just looking at Hasan's nervous face I knew things were tense. I felt kind of bad for him. It really wasn't his fault. If Tapoti hadn't shown so much confidence I would have never allowed two inexperienced persons to paddle the boat.

" Why are you just looking? Do something." Shili was getting impatient.

Jerin bhabi was at the verge of breakdown. " How could you let my two jewels go with that mad man? Who knows where the boat would end up floating? Can't you do anything to save them? "

Still not sensing any real urgency I understood I had to take some measures or I could end up in bigger trouble for just being on the shore. I tried to attract their attention by waving and yelling at the top of my voice. Once getting their attention I tried to give them a lesson on rowing as I noticed they were rowing incoherently resulting into the uncontrolled drift. After several minute of shouting back and forth I had to stop as it wasn't going anywhere. Hasan and Tapoti tried their best to follow but neither the spin ceased nor the drifting.

At this point I first noticed the crowd that had gathered along the shore to enjoy the show. Most clearly did not consider the situation to be serious as they laughed and chatted. A few video cameras were yanked out of their bags and turned on. It won't be a surprise if this whole thing was uploaded in the internet. Now a day's a video of somebody sneezing can become sensational and get a million hits.

Helpless, I went to rent a boat. Unfortunately the stall had just closed. Luckily few of the park employees from the stall were still in the area. I asked them for help and learned that in situations like this a formal rescue team must be disbursed. They had a motor boat to be used for rescue missions. However we would have to wait as the crew had another more urgent task in hand. It was such a beautiful summer day that people had crowded the park in exceptionally large numbers. As a result a pipe broke in the public washroom flooding it. They needed to take care of that first. The trio sitting on the boat looked healthy and secured inside their life jackets. There didn't seem to have any immediate need for them to be rescued.

The park crew left one guy behind to bring the rescue boat down to the water. Once returned they would attach the motor and off would they go.

"What kind of people are they?" Jerin bhabi bitterly said. "How could they just leave like that when two kids are in such danger? Brother, why aren't you doing something?"

I tried to soothe her with my best smile. "Don't be so worried. What's the worst can happen? They would float to the other side."

"Then?"

"Our rescue team would go and rescue them. Bhabi, you are worrying for nothing. Everything will be fine."

"I wish you had some common sense." She blasted. "What do they know of rowing a boat? How could you let them go all by themselves? Shame on you!"

"Now you know, bhabi." Shili added, hinting how irresponsible I was in everything I did making her life so miserable.

I gave her a nasty look, at least tried my best. What the world is turning into? Nobody let go any opportunity to demean others.

Hasan and Tapoti had given the rowing a little rest. After a few minutes rest they had picked up the oars again and were paddling around the boat vigorously. As both of them paddled in random directions the boat had little choice but to simply spin. I shouted asking one of them to stop. They misunderstood me. The rate of paddling increased.

"It's better if you didn't say anything at all,

brother." Jerin bhai bitterly said. "Every time you say something things are turning worse."

I kept quite. Who had dreamt something like this could even happen? I noticed the current was getting stronger in McLaughlin bay which worked slightly in our favor as it started to push the boat toward the shore on the other side. However, I was doubtful how much help that would be as the shoreline on that side were forested and had no proper opening to climb out of the boat. Yet the depth of the water was less near the shore and so was the current reducing the risk of drifting away into the deeper water. Nevertheless waiting too long to rescue them seemed like a poor choice and I felt quite annoyed thinking of all days the flooding in the washrooms had to happen today and that also around the same time when we needed some help.

The park crew returned after about twenty minutes. The flooding wasn't as bad as it sounded. They left one person behind to handle it and returned for the rescue job. It was a big relief. They struggled a little bit to carry the heavy engine from the boathouse to the boat and get it placed properly. The main problem however, started when they tried to get the engine going which obviously would roar and gargle but won't start. That definitely wasn't something that the hundreds of spectators who had waited patiently had expected. Naturally nobody was happy. A deluge of sarcasm headed toward the nervous and anxious crew.

"What a rescue team!" Somebody joked with the crowd cackling.

"We'll need another rescue team to rescue this team." Somebody else added with the crowd bursting into laughter.

It kept on coming with people becoming more creative.

Around this time I noticed Tapoti had had enough by now with paddling and she had taken her oar out of the water, waiting for the rescue to happen. Hasan was not about to give up. He continued to paddle and owing to some magical forces managed to guide the boat near the opposite shore. Of course they were still not in any position to get out of that wretched thing but at least they were now in shallower water. This achievement must had had been quite pleasing to Hasan because he was grinning contently.

Jerin bhabi went berserk. "Look who is smiling! Doesn't he have any shame? One million people are standing here watching this drama, some are also recording, and he is smiling! Shame! Shame!"

I had to struggle to keep myself from chuckling. I had no desire to become the next target of her resentment. Our rescue team had been trying diligently to get the engine going. Who knew why, perhaps just to make the crowd happy, the engine finally roared into life. The crowd applauded loudly as the young crew blushed. It was quite clear that they had not ever been involved into such rescue effort. This was safe water and I doubted anybody really needed a true rescue mission here. .

It wasn't before another five minutes had passed that our rescue team completed their routine checks as per preset protocol and moved ahead. This resulted in a sarcastic applaud and another round of sarcasms - apparently lead by some of the elderly ladies who had gathered.

"Let's pray that the rescue boat don't get turn over mid river. What a wreck!"

The crowd roared into laughter. In a nice late afternoon coupled with a comfortable breeze from the lake most people must have been feeling quite relaxed, especially realizing it was all about to end in a good note. Jerin bhabi gave them a hard look.

"I can't believe how heartless these people are! Why are they laughing? My two children are floating away who knows where and these rascals are laughing their heads off! Shame! Shame!"

Everything is well that ends well. The three member rescue team of ours hooked up the inflatable boat and started to pull it back to safety. Jerin bhabi, heavily relieved, brought out all kind of cameras from her carry-on bag and started to take snapshots and videos in plentiful. She was an avid member of Facebook and it took no telling where all these images and videos were going to end up.

"I told you everything will be fine." I took this opportunity to tease her. "What were you so upset about? Look, they are all in one piece."

"Thanks god, I got my kids back." She could barely resist her joy.

"How about the daddy? You are not happy about him?" I joked.

She rolled her eyes. "After all the embarrassment he caused? He can stay in that boat."

I restrained myself from extending that conversation. The embarrassment part could not be ignored. The rescue boat returned to the dock with my poor inflatable on the tow. I helped the inflatable to a shallow section where Hasan and the kids could step out on the ground without getting wet. Once on his feet - safe and sound - Hasan was quick to brush away all the embarrassment. He even went on to mention," We were doing just fine. There was no need to send the rescue team."

I thought it would be Jerin bhabi who would give him what he deserved. Not so. It was Tapoti who barked," After all these years you still don't know how to manage a small boat. What a total loser you are!"

The End